# THE BALLAD OF
# BLACK BART

# BOOKS BY LOREN D. ESTLEMAN

*Published by Tom Doherty Associates

# THE BALLAD
★★★ OF ★★★
# BLACK BART

## LOREN D. ESTLEMAN

A TOM DOHERTY ASSOCIATES BOOK  NEW YORK

THE BALLAD OF BLACK BART

Copyright © 2017 by Loren D. Estleman

A Forge Book
Published by Tom Doherty Associates
175 Fifth Avenue
New York, NY 10010

www.tor-forge.com

Forge® is a registered trademark of Macmillan Publishing Group, LLC.

The Library of Congress Cataloging-in-Publication Data is available
upon request.

ISBN 978-0-7653-8353-2 (hardcover)
ISBN 978-1-4668-9211-8 (ebook)

Our books may be purchased in bulk for promotional, educational,
or business use. Please contact your local bookseller or the
Macmillan Corporate and Premium Sales Department
at 1-800-221-7945, extension 5442, or by email at
MacmillanSpecialMarkets@macmillan.com.

First Edition: November 2017

Printed in the United States of America

0  9  8  7  6  5  4  3  2  1

To the memory of Matt Braun:
such artists come a thousand years apart;
such friends but once;

and

To the memory of Lenore Carroll:
a woman of brilliant mind, beautiful nature,
and dauntless courage

*'Twas a thief said the last kind word to Christ.*
*Christ took the kindness and forgave the theft.*

—**Robert Browning**

# I

# SHANK'S MARE

*The stars look very cold about the sky,*
*and I have many miles on foot to fare.*

**—John Keats**

# ONE

*This is the story of bandit Black Bart;*
*who used the gold country to practice his art.*
*His brush was a shotgun, his canvas the road,*
*as he painted his way 'cross the Old Mother Lode.*

ho do you like in the fight, Charlie?" Matt Leacock
asked.

The gentleman seated across the table in the restaurant's small dining room smiled; at least his handsome set of salt-and-pepper handlebars lifted at the corners. He wasn't a grinner, showing pleasure only when something amused him. It struck Leacock that to him, Nob Hill's gang of glad-handers must look like gibbering monkeys. "What fight is that, Matt?" Charlie asked.

"Any fight; or the ponies. You've usually got something down on one or the other."

"Now, if I was to tell you that, and you put any store in my judgment, the odds just might shoot north of Sacramento, and where would that leave me? On the short end."

The third man at the table, Alec Fitzhugh, chuckled. He had his linen napkin tucked under his cutthroat collar and both hands busy cutting his prime rib into bite-size pieces, each one as red as a penny poker chip. "You are a close-mouthed man. I don't guess you would unbend far enough to tell me how you like the oysters."

"A mite chewy, since you ask." Charles Bolton slid a raw quivering lump of mollusk off the edge of a half-shell into his mouth, nibbled briefly, and swallowed, chasing it with mineral water. He ate more daintily with his hands than his companions did with knives and forks. He seldom had use for the napkin in his lap. "If it's your intention to invest beyond beef, I would avoid the market in seafood this season."

His listeners' amusement was leavened with thoughtful self-interest. The fellow from New York (or was it Boston? He was as tight with autobiographical detail as he was with general information) had a reputation for answering even a casual inquiry with an air of gravity, as if he'd given the matter a world of thought before committing himself to a response.

Everything about this man was reserved, from his table manners to his conversation to his dress, blacks and grays mostly, with a brief burst of green satin where the knot of his cravat nestled between the lapels of his double-breasted waistcoat. In San Francisco, whose mining barons, textile magnates, and dry-goods kings had made their fortunes off the rip-roaring camps of the Forty-Niners (and now from their widows), loud talk, fat cigars, and whiskey flasks the size of cavalry canteens were the norm. A man who drank rarely, smoked not at all, and spent his words as if they as-sayed out at sixteen dollars to the ounce, was regarded as some kind of sage. But for the chin-whiskers and pale blue eyes, Charles Bolton might have posed for the cedar red man standing sentry outside every tobacco shop in the U.S.

Leacock added a dollop of brandy from the cut-glass decanter to the milk in his glass. He suffered from the successful businessman's twin complaints, ulcers and gout, but also his disdain for absolute temperance. "I've noticed you don't spend much time around other mining men, Charlie. I make my living shipping cattle to the slaughteryards in Chicago, and Alec lights the lamps of New York City with whale blubber. Do you not like the company you used to keep?"

"I cast no aspersions on them. The last thing I want when I'm through inspecting the fields is shop talk." Bolton pushed away his plate of plundered shells and sat back, cradling his glass as carefully as if it contained French champagne. "I think from time to time of investing in the moneymaking end of the race game," he told Leacock. "Buy a nag of my own and run it round the circuit. What do you think?"

Leacock started to smile, but adjusted himself to the company. "I guess I've breathed in enough sweat off the tramps who ride the damn beasts to the railhead, and dropped enough at the track, to know a horse is good for only two things, raising blisters and running dead last. What do you want with those hay-burners anyway, Charlie? You can lose money just as fast on a sporting woman, and you don't have to feed her."

"I don't appreciate that kind of talk." Bolton rolled the glass between his palms, then moved a shoulder. "But I thank you for the counsel. I never had much use for the animal myself. Most places I go, I walk."

Fitzhugh frowned, dipped his napkin in his own water glass, and rubbed at a fresh stain on his shirtboard. "No one walks in this town, Charlie. That's what cable cars are for."

"God gave men legs for a reason. I reckon I will keep using mine till He tells me different."

A strange thing to say, Leacock thought, considering the man's obvious affliction.

Bolton stirred himself, as if the conversation were becoming uncomfortable. More likely he was bored. Truth be told, he seemed to have little in common with his companions except the incapacity to show concern when the check came. He separated a pair of notes from his soft kidskin wallet, laid them on the brass tray the waiter had brought, and rose, shaking hands with the others. "Good night, gentlemen."

"Odd fellow," said Fitzhugh, after he'd left.

"And not much of a tipper." Leacock finished counting the notes in the tray and laid them back down.

"They say the same about Vanderbilt."

Charles Bolton waited behind another patron before the check room, shifting his weight painfully from one foot to the other. The man was complaining about a pair of gloves missing from his coat pocket. Finally he left, and Bolton stirred his moustaches for the young lady behind the desk. She wore her hair in sausage curls and an ankle-length white apron, like a Harvey girl, and was flushed from the contentious encounter. She smiled in happy recognition and retrieved Bolton's Chesterfield overcoat and brushed bowler without asking for his check. He accepted them and handed her a nickel from the change pocket of his wallet, which bulged with notes.

She braved a smile. "Anything else, Mr. Bolton?"

He smiled back. This girl, so pale and quick to blush, brought him joy. From the wallet he produced a fold of foolscap and passed it across the desk.

She unfolded it and read silently, her lips moving:

> The versers pick their subjects, from urns to birds
> to oak; but the one I'd place my name to is the girl
> who checks my cloak.

Her cheeks flushed bright. "How wonderful! You should be a poet."

"Were I twenty years younger; and you of age."

She folded the poem into her apron pocket. "You know, you shouldn't carry so much cash around, Mr. Bolton. San Francisco isn't New York City."

"New York's no different, only a little bigger. I don't trust banks."

"Are you worried about Jesse James?"

His gentle face broke into creases. "A common thief? He isn't worth my time."

"The papers don't think he's common."

"Charge into a bank, shoot up everyone between you and the money, and gallop on out, gunning down strangers and trampling children in the street? I find that all *too* common."

"You're right, of course. If only everyone were as civilized as you."

He walked the few blocks to Post Street and the Webb House, a small, well-ordered establishment with a shallow lobby containing a rubber tree in a bronze pot and a scrap of Persian rug. The half-caste Chinese behind the carved desk handed him his key without being asked.

"Can you have the girl bring up a bucket of hot water?"

"Certainly, sir."

Bolton thanked him and ascended the broad floral-carpeted stairs to the second floor, leaning a little on the banisters; his feet were giving him more than usual discomfort. He blamed the oysters.

In his room, a comfortable corner one with a brass bed, a bath adjoining, and a pitcher and basin, he sat in the horsehair armchair and pulled off his boots, carefully peeling them away where he'd made cuts to accommodate his corns. When the knock came he shambled over in his stockings and opened the door for the old Chinese woman to come in and fill the basin with steaming water from her bucket. Her eyes brightened in their thicket of wrinkles when he gave her a dime for the effort.

Alone again, he knelt to slide his valise, a fine pale pigskin satchel turning brown at the corners, from under the bed and opened it on the mattress to extract a shotgun, sawed off to two feet and wrapped in an oily rag. His big toes when he rolled his socks off were less swollen than earlier in the week, thanks to his daily soakings. Perched on the edge of the bed and hissing through his teeth, he lowered his feet into the hot water. Sweat broke out on his forehead as he waited for them to adjust to the scald. After a few moments, the heat soothed, drawing the residual pain off toward the edges of the basin and away. There he sat until the water grew lukewarm. Waiting, he wiped down the shotgun with the oily rag, then set it aside and drew a sheet of stiff paper from the nightstand's marble top.

It was a stagecoach passenger's schedule, listing routes for the month of August 1877. He came to one beginning in Point Arena, terminating in Duncan Mills, and running through Sonoma County and climbing the foothills near the Russian River. Drawing a carpenter's pencil from his waistcoat pocket, he circled this, then selected a map from the stack on the nightstand and spread it open beside him. The road passed south of old Fort Ross. He licked the pencil's blunt tip, then circled this too, singing under his breath:

> Come listen to my story, I'll not detain you long.
> A singing and a humming this simple silly song.
> 'Tis of the old ex-convicts,
> the men who served their time
> for robbing mountain stages of the Wells, Fargo
> line.

# TWO

*Now, Bart used no horses to gather his loot.*
*He held them a bother, and bad luck to boot.*
*So he trod California noons, evenings, and morns,*
*bathing his bunions and cursing his corns.*

He ate breakfast at daybreak and asked the waitress to prepare a bacon sandwich to take with him. She did so, between two thick slices of coarse sourdough bread, wrapped in a page of *The Sacramento Bee*. He put the parcel in a pocket of the sturdy miner's overalls he wore under his traveling duster, gave her an extra nickel for her trouble, and picked up his blanket roll. She noticed the twin barrels of a shotgun poking out the end. "The grouse are in good supply this year," she said.

"I aim to whittle down the population."

It was a fine day for a walk. August is a mild month in northern California, and the sun lay across his shoulders like a shawl. From time to time he changed hands on the blanket roll, heavy with the shotgun, a hatchet, and a full canteen. Such travelers as he encountered on the road out-side town—people riding in carriages and buckboards and the occasional man on horseback—exchanged nods with the middle-aged man out rusticating, and if they noticed his weapon they assumed he was either hunting small game or prepared to defend himself against highwaymen. The stage roads in the locality provided the main route for gold dust on its way to the assay offices in Sacramento and, converted into notes, to the banks. Those who preyed on the coaches seldom bothered with individuals, but one could never be too cautious in mining territory.

By noon, he felt the first twinges in his feet, but kept going until he arrived at the spot identified on his map as Meyers Grade, with Fort Ross, deserted since the cessation of hostilities between eastern settlers, coastal Indians, and Russian poachers, five miles to the north. There he spread out his roll, took out its contents and laid them aside, folded the blanket, and sat on it to strip off his boots and stockings. He lowered both feet into a mountain stream so icy he felt the cold all the way to his teeth. He sighed relief, unwrapped his sandwich, and ate it, drinking from the canteen and reading a week-old news item stained with grease, headed ROUGH JUSTICE.

A man in Fresno had spoken too freely of his neighbors' wives and been hung by his heels by a gang of masked men in consequence. He was rescued some hours later on the verge of death, but was not expected to recover. Swift punishment was promised for the vigilantes.

Which pledge would be the end of the affair, and well served. Bolton shook his head and used a dry corner of the paper to wipe grease from his moustaches.

A few yards upstream, an ungainly looking bird, its head too big for its body and its feet too small, plunged from its

station on a branch overhanging the water. It vanished below the surface less than half a second, then with an explo-
sion of flapping wings emerged with a yellow perch clamped
in its needlelike bill. Struggling against the fish's frantic
resistance, it staggered on its cripple's feet to a flat rock and
smacked its catch repeatedly against the stone until it stopped
thrashing. Then the bird began eating, snatching up quivering chunks of flesh and jerking them down its throat.

"They don't call you kingfisher for nothing," Bolton said.

The bird paid him no attention, concentrating on its
meal.

When it had eaten its fill and flown off, Bolton dried his
feet with a handkerchief, put on his stockings and boots,
crumpled the newspaper, buried it a few inches deep in the
loose earth, and rose, rewrapping the canteen, hatchet, and
shotgun, and picking up the roll.

The hill was everything he'd hoped, an inclined plane
falling away steeply from where he stood, on a foundation
of powdery red dust topped with a spill of pebbles and glittering shards of quartz: bonanza country, built on shifting
sand by the patron saint of prospectors and pirates; especially pirates. Any horsedrawn vehicle would have to slow
to a crawl to make the grade.

Shielding his eyes with his free hand, he noted the sun's
position, confirmed the time by his turnip watch, and went
to work.

He took out the hatchet, chopped four branches off a cottonwood, about an inch and a half in diameter, three feet
long, and as straight as they grew, making the cuts square
and stripping off the leaves with a clasp knife. He trimmed
off the twigs and leaves and wedged one end of each between

two rocks, one rock stacked on the other, spacing them a few yards apart, with the cut ends pointing down the slope. After examining the result, he repositioned one of the branches, stepped back for another look, and deemed himself satisfied. Then he bundled up his tools and descended, clutching striplings and handfuls of scrub on the way to maintain his balance. At a semi-level spot near the halfway point he turned and looked up the hill, reassuring himself as to the arrangement of the branches: four narrow cylinders with their ends tilted in toward that section of road.

He was ahead of schedule, having allowed for the unexpected and also the necessary periods of repose. He found a comfortable depression behind a large boulder on the side of the hill, spread the blanket again, and assumed a half-reclining position on the soft earth, propping his boots up on a smaller boulder, the shotgun across his lap and his bowler tipped forward over his eyes. In a little while the grosbeaks and flickers, who had ceased singing when the man appeared, dismissed him as a threat and resumed their warbling and wick-wicking.

The stage was late, but not excessively so; the driver would make up the difference on the flat. Bolton heard it coming for a mile, its harness rings jingling and the mud wagon creaking on its stiff leather straps, the wheels grinding through gravel, manufacturing yet more dust, and the driver shouting those singsong imprecations that any good team reacted to as if they were gentle encouragement.

As the noise increased, reverberating off the trunks of the titanic redwoods walling the sides of the road, he stood, working the kinks out of his muscles and pronouncing his feet sound, and took a flour sack from his bib pocket. He drew it over his head, hat and all, adjusted the holes he'd cut to line up with his eyes, and breathed in that smell of stone-ground grain that made his heart pound every time he came across it, even walking past a grist mill in the pose of Charles E. Bolton, mining magnate. The shotgun was a comforting weight in his hands.

The coach—built light like a military ambulance, with open sides and mounted for stability rather than convenience—was good enough for rough country, if nowhere near as comfortable or impressive as the fabled red-painted Concord, with its cradle-like suspension and dust-resistant side curtains. The driver was alone on the seat. No shotgun messenger meant nothing like a large shipment of gold dust; but Wells, Fargo barely broke even on fares. There would be enough in the express box to make this worthwhile, and less risk.

Over his boulder, the man in the flour sack noted that more effort had gone into the team's selection than its burden. The Company reserved these handsome matched mounts for the first and last legs of the journey, to impress onlookers in town: One set for Point Arena, stamping and blowing before the station, another flexing its sleek, egg-shaped muscles on the way to the stable in the thriving lumber town of Duncan Mills. In between, slat-sided glue-pots selected more for endurance than beauty, with few witnesses to express disappointment at their fistulas and hollow grass-fed flanks. The frugality of Henry Wells and William Fargo was nearly as infamous as their business practices.

"The bastards," Bolton said under his breath. He never cursed within anyone's earshot.

The coach began its long climb, the horses blowing from the effort, slowing as their hooves churned up earth the color of dried blood and ground fine as flour. The man in the mask bent his knees, took a deep breath, and sprang out into the middle of the road, canting his shotgun up toward the driver's seat and thumbing back both hammers with a noise like walnut shells cracking. The lead horses shied, tossing their heads and planting their hooves in the gravel, throwing dust that drifted back over their shoulders and settled on the boots of the man gripping the lines. Instinctively he hauled back with all his weight, as if the brutes needed the incentive to stop. There followed a creaking and groaning of wood, leather, and luggage lashed to the top and stored in the boot coming to the end of their forward momentum without warning.

The driver, milk-glass pale behind his moustaches and sunburn, wrestled with the team's panic, sawing the lines and hissing between his teeth. The man in the flour sack gave him time to settle the horses down, then gestured with the shotgun toward the ironbound strongbox at the driver's feet. "Please throw down the box."

The driver hesitated, looking down the shining twin barrels, then stooped, grasped the leather handles of the green-painted box, lifted it grunting, and threw it over the side. It struck the earth and laid without bouncing, as if it contained an anvil or something equally heavy.

The masked man turned his head toward the top of the hill. "If he makes a move, give him a volley, boys."

The driver followed his gaze, toward what were certainly four rifle barrels trained on him from behind a string of boulders. He raised his gloved palms to the level of his shoulders.

In that country, a noise from a coach suspended on straps carried as far as a crack of thunder. Flour Sack swung his shotgun toward the passenger compartment, which was packed full, just as an arm—a woman's, from the lace at the cuff—reached through the opening on his side of the vehicle and dropped a floral-embroidered reticule into the dust. Cradling the shotgun in the crook of his arm with the barrels pointed toward the driver, the man in the flour sack bent, scooped up the handbag, and tossed it back through the window.

"Madam, I do not wish your money. In that respect, I honor only the good office of Wells, Fargo."

He stepped off the road, sweeping a hand toward the top of the hill. The driver snapped his lines and the team resumed its climb. Nearing the crest, he chanced a glance toward the riflemen, but there was no sign of them, and the rifles looked suspiciously like something harmless.

But the "rifles" and the man in the sack were no longer any of Ash Wilkinson's concern. The veteran driver snatched his bullwhip from its socket and unfurled it over the lead horses' heads, hell-bent for leather for Duncan Mills and the disapproving face of the stage agent there, but with his passengers' lives—and more particularly his own—intact.

When the jingling and rattling faded into the day-to-day sounds of the wilderness, indicating that their master had no intention of circling back, Charles Bolton swung the hatchet. Two sharp blows separated the padlock from the hasp. He wasted no time distributing three hundred dollars in gold double eagles among his various pockets; not much of a windfall as robberies went, but six months' pay by most standards, and no one would question them in his bank in San Francisco, not from a gentleman who did regular business there and dressed accordingly to the time and place.

A mailbag, slashed open, yielded nothing more interesting than a bank draft for a similar amount. This too he pocketed; he was loath to leave behind anything of potential value. Later he would discard the check as too dangerous to attempt to turn into cash.

A Company waybill lay inside the strongbox. He took it out and kicked the empty box off the road. Smiling, he licked the tip of his carpenter's pencil, stared for a moment at blue sky pushing between redwood branches far above his head, then scribbled on the back of the waybill. He read what he'd written and added a line to the bottom before picking up his shotgun and walking in the opposite direction of the way he'd come, whistling "The Wells, Fargo Line."

Hours later, a party of lawmen and volunteers from Duncan Mills saw paper flapping and found the note atop a blackened fir stump, weighted down with a rock.

*I've labored long for bread*
*for honor and for riches,*
*but on my corns too long you've tread*
*you fine-haired Sons of Bitches.*

—Black Bart, the Po8

# THREE

*Thieves as a rule leave their victims bereft;*
*marooned and abandoned, and with nothing left.*
*But Bart wasn't like that, to be so unfair;*
*he left them a verse to help ease their despair.*

It was a trek back to San Francisco, and no mistake; a younger man with fewer physical challenges would not have attempted it. But good Samaritans spared him the worst of it, and his feet weren't as bad as he made out for the benefit of his companions and the hotel staff in San Francisco. Better to let on that he was unequal to a long walk than for others to guess that long walks—long, *long*, Homeric walks—were the source of his miseries. Shank's mare left fewer traces than iron-shod hooves, and the dense woodlands were easier for a pedestrian seeking cover from suspicious strangers than a rider on horseback; he could slide between the trees like mountain runoff. When one chose the path he had, the dangers doubled, from both the law and the ruffians who'd turned the coach roads into their personal hunting field. He didn't place himself among that class, notwithstanding the gold coins bagging all his pockets.

When he was relatively certain he wasn't under immediate pursuit, he turned off the path and rested, resisting the temptation to remove his boots and massage his stockinged soles. There was nothing more preposterous than to be surprised discalced, and attempt to escape carrying his boots in one hand and yelping at pebbles, like the Other Man fleeing a bedroom in a rude joke.

Ten miles farther on, with dusk sifting down, he turned in at a warmly lit cabin, occupied by a settler and his wife, who farmed and did a little prospecting, which they said supplemented them from time to time with a pinch of dust here and a tiny nugget there. They noted his worn boots and rough clothing and took him for an itinerant, a common sight since the Panic, who entertained them over a simple but nourishing dinner with tales he'd collected while hiking and riding the rails. He slept on a cot in the pantry—dug into the hillside to preserve potatoes and goods canned in jars—wrapped in his blanket against the cold, and was gone by daybreak.

The desk man at the Webb—not the half-caste who stood there afternoons and evenings—recognized the weary man hobbling in at midmorning, and produced his key.

"Out checking your holdings again, Mr. Bolton?"

He nodded without elaborating, and asked for a bucket of hot water. The clerk made a sympathetic face; and this time the guest's discomfort was not exaggerated.

\* \* \*

James Hume grunted through his handlebars at the paper in his hand. "He's not precisely the Bard, is he?"

THE BALLAD OF BLACK BART ★ 29

Sheriff Thorn fingered his spade-shaped beard, streaked with silver. "I wouldn't know. It sure sticks in the craw."

Wells, Fargo, & Co. maintained two narrow stories of brick construction on Montgomery Street, a neighborhood which was still referred to by longtime San Franciscans as the Fireproof Block, even though most of the city now was built of the same durable materials intended to put an end to the fires that had burned it to the ground times without number. The building, sturdy but unprepossessing, represented the nerve center of a national freighting firm as self-contained as any great city, with its own police force, telegraph offices, fleet of rolling stock and, in the person of Chief of Detectives James Hume, a Department of War.

His office was small by such lofty standards: a cedar-paneled box with a window overlooking the constant horsedrawn traffic twelve feet below. It looked like the inside of a humidor and smelled like one, from the cedar and from cigars smoked, discarded, and replaced, as many as the ghosts of Gettysburg. Hume kept open the window and shutters, both to vent the exhaust and to encourage the intoxicating stimulation of loud industry from the noisiest city west of Chicago.

The building was four times as deep as it was wide, extending back a city block. In the adjoining offices, rows of oaken file cases contained the records of every transaction conducted by Wells, Fargo, and every assault upon it by road agents, including three committed by a polite-spoken man wearing a flour sack over his head, but no name as yet.

Until yesterday.

A parchment-colored map of California's gold country,

all the towns and features lettered in copperplate, hung behind Hume's desk in a rustic twig frame. Pins with yellow flags marked the sites of recent stagecoach robberies; the roads through California's Mother Lode country alone resembled a daisy festival. That patch of real property was the latest and liveliest in a long line of Robbers Roosts, stretching nearly as far back as Sutter's Mill. This Black Bart might have drawn straws with the competition for the opportunity.

As if to remind Hume of his responsibilities, portraits of Henry Wells and William G. Fargo glowered at him from behind their full beards on opposite sides of the map. Their likenesses might have been lithographed on a tin of cough drops.

"Same procedure as Calaveras," Hume told Sheriff Benjamin Thorn. "That's why I called you in out of your jurisdiction."

"Nevada County, too, and Cottonwood." Thorn lifted the empty mailbag the Sonoma County authorities had recovered, with its distinctive T-shaped slash. "Same cut, same description."

Hume held up the waybill. "Do the journals have this?"

"Not to my knowledge, but you never know when one of the rascals might arrange to have himself swept up in the call for volunteers. There ought to be a law requiring them to wear uniforms, so we can tell them from people."

"One enemy at a time, Ben. I'll put something together when they come nosing around, and issue a reward bulletin, strictly for professionals, and hope to keep Mr. Bart's literary aspirations to ourselves. I'll thank you and your people to play it as close."

"I ain't green, Jim. I've worn this star a mite longer than you did before they tapped you for this job."

Hume rotated his cigar, in an effort to make it burn more evenly as he puffed. His colleague in office was a first-class lawman, but as a politician his judgment was suspect; witness that colossus of brick and stone he shared with his family in San Andreas, so large and rambling the cynical electorate had dubbed it the "Thorn Mansion," surely the most ostentatious dwelling any public servant ever maintained, honest or otherwise.

Despite such doubts, the voters had kept him in office for fifteen years—in his profession, a lifetime west of St. Louis—demonstrating in effect a higher regard for efficiency than for probity. Thorn had grown gray in a job that turned most men out—quit, ousted, or killed—before thirty. The man delivered, rain or shine, with an eagle eye for physical evidence and the memory of an elephant: His very presence on the witness stand was as good as a conviction. Who troubled to count the number of chimney pots he owned, or cared whether they were swept clean and at what cost, so long as the peace was maintained? When such men came into Hume's orbit, the devil take the rest.

And there was something to be said for hunting with a terrier who was himself part weasel.

"Mr. Valentine never stood on our side of the star," Hume said. "He was born a superintendent, with a pencil behind his ear, and bleeds red and black ink. When he asks did I bring up the subject of public notoriety, I intend to tell the truth. He would rather take the loss than waste good men over three hundred dollars, but those press fellows get as hot and bothered as any sourdough over the slightest trace of color. If it got out that this fellow thumbed his nose at the Company—in impertinent rhyme, no less—and we didn't crush him on the spot, we might as well issue an invitation to every road agent between Canada and old Mexico to come rob us." He puffed a cloud in the direction of the ceiling, stained coppery with nicotine. "Trying to track one man, in all those canyons and gulches, with every journal in the country nipping at our heels? As well chase a feather in a cyclone."

"If one line of that poim makes its way into print, by God, I will track down the man responsible and clap him in irons."

"You do that, Ben, if you want to see this Black Bart plastered all over *Harper's Weekly*. Those ink-slingers do circle their wagons. Come next election you'll be taking in boarders in that palace of yours."

"Aw, Jim, you know I paid for it out of the commission the county pays me for collecting the tax."

"Ben, I don't care. I live in San Mateo."

The sheriff was in no wise mollified, but let the matter drop. "I am just a policeman, with twelve deputies and a turnkey to keep the peace over a jurisdiction the size of Scotland. With Wells, Fargo at your back and your own past history, Jim, there's no reason you won't have this tin-pot versifier behind bars before the scribbling bastards find out about it."

Compliments, even genuine ones, annoyed the detective. He never responded to them one way or the other, except to note that his salary had been increased from time to time. He glanced at the poem once more, then scaled it to the top of the heap of leather-bound portfolios and loose papers on his desk. "Let's see that stick."

The pair shared a passion for details. Thorn's Sonoma colleagues and volunteers had recovered one of the fir branches the bandit had arranged to gull the coachman into thinking he was sitting in the center of a field of fire. He passed it across the desk, taking care to avoid upsetting the tray of ashes and butts balanced on top of the slag.

Hume examined each end, testing it with a thumb. "Used the hatchet he broke open the box with to cut it free, and a knife with a small blade to strip it and carve the other end to look like a rifle bore, just like the others. The man's clever."

"Clever enough to overstep himself. Sooner or later he'll brag himself up over a bottle in the Bella Union or some-such place and we'll snatch him on the spot. My men visit all the gin-houses in Barbary."

"I reckon you don't lack for volunteers." No smile stirred Hume's moustaches. "I doubt it will be that easy. If he were so reckless, he wouldn't work alone. How did he get there, and away?"

"By horse, same as everyone else."

"You talked to the witnesses. No one saw him mount up."

"You know how it is with witnesses. Next week they'll say he stood an Arabian on its hind legs and stitched his name into a tree trunk with a forty-four, like Deadwood Dick."

"So far they've all agreed on the description: medium height and build, straight back, soft-spoken."

"They did that. It suits you, Jim, as much as anyone. Where was *you* yesterday afternoon?"

The detective ignored that. His sense of humor ran neck-and-neck with his regard for accolades. "He must have broke winged Pegasus to make away without leaving hoofprints. If you ask my opinion, I'd say he travels afoot."

"A *walking* bandit? Who ever heard of such a thing?"

"It's not so much of a stretch, Ben. Yesterday morning no one ever heard of a highwayman who writes poetry."

# FOUR

*A fox is too crafty for most barnyard stock,*
*so they hired a rooster what crossed with a hawk.*
*Jim Hume was a hunter of men, so they say,*
*more than equipped to put Black Bart at bay.*

Despite the success of its freight and passenger operations, Wells, Fargo, & Co. considered itself first and foremost a bank, and the ground floor of its building in San Francisco was typical of that field of commerce, with varnished oak cages to protect the tellers from daylight robbery—America's fastest-growing enterprise—pens chained to inkwells, and the inevitable line of customers waiting their turn before the single cage that was open at that time of day.

The incident here related could have happened.

After leaving Hume's office, Sheriff Thorn came down the stairwell and held open the street door for a new arrival. The man, of medium height and build, wearing a satin-faced chesterfield, touched the brim of his bowler in thanks and took his place in line. Thorn went out.

The teller smiled. He was clean-shaven and balding, in a morning coat and stiff collar. "Another deposit, Mr. Spaulding? Perhaps I should buy shares."

Bolton smiled. It pleased him to maintain an account under a fictitious name in Wells, Fargo's own safe.

"I'd not, Mr. Pincus. You were in knickerbockers when I started digging. I shouldn't wish to tot it up by the hour. Just an exchange today. Dollar notes, and a small draft." He slid a sheet of Webb House stationery under the cage with the figure $4.25 written on it in coarse pencil.

When the teller finished changing two twenty-dollar coins into notes and silver and drawing the draft, Bolton pocketed his cash, including seventy-five cents in change, and stepped to a stand-up desk in the corner. There he unfolded a cutting from a pocket. On thin newsprint was a lithographic image of a low-cut boot, square-toed, with elastic sides. The copy, in a bold font, read:

### MEN'S BOX ANKLE-HIGH CUT
### STORM SHOE

**THE SHOE** which we herewith illustrate is one of the most desirable of the new styles available, for Fall and Winter wear, and in fact is a splendid choice regardless of the season. We build this shoe with heavy soles and full outside extension, for hard wear.

**SIZES AND HALF SIZES, 5 TO 11**

**WIDTHS C, D, AND EE**

For postage rates, see page 4.

Per pair,

$2.75.

He confirmed the $1.50 shipping charge scribbled in the margin, enclosed the cutting and the blank on which he'd written his shoe size and hotel address, sealed them with the draft in a Webb envelope, dipped a pen, and addressed it to Montgomery Ward & Co., 246-254 Kinzie St., Chicago, Ill. Then he walked down the street on run-down heels to stamp and post it.

\* \* \*

On the second floor—a dozen feet above Black Bart's head, if we accept the foregoing as truth—James Hume lit a fresh cigar and took a typewritten sheet from Jonathan Thacker, his aide and secretary, who shared the small office, with his Remington Visible Writing Machine propped on a plain table placed strategically to allow room to pass between it and the detective chief's desk and to avoid being bumped by the door when it was opened. The copy was neat, with no strike-overs:

$800 Reward!
ARREST STAGE ROBBER!
On the 3rd of August, 1877, the stage from Fort Ross
to the Russian River was stopped by one man, who
took from the Express box about $300, coin...On one
of the Way Bills left with the box the writer wrote
as follows:

Black Bart's impudent poem was centered.

More details were included.

Hume, a methodical man, read through it twice, top to bottom, then off-loaded a pile of papers to another stack, exposing a brass inkstand from which he drew a horsehair pen and added to the top of the page in a hand nearly as tidy as the typed characters:

> Agents of W., F. & Co. will not post this circular to the public, but place it in the hands of officers and reliable citizens in your region. Officers and citizens receiving them are requested to preserve them for future reference.

"I'll leave it to their discretion to decide reliability." He returned the sheet to the young man in shirtsleeves and green velvet sleeve protectors. "The trail's muddy enough without an army of bounty rats trampling it further."

"Yes, sir."

"Come back with a galley sheet as soon as it's ready. The printer is not to proceed until I initial it."

The secretary smiled. "We can't have him select a nine instead of an eight from the typecase. Bad enough we're offering five hundred more than the ruffian took in cash."

"I'll thank you not to question the methods of your betters."

The young man flushed deeply and departed, leaving the door open to the exhilarating din from outside.

Immediately upon his exit, Hume's face lightened a shade.

*Millions for defense,* he thought, drawing on the cigar, *but not one cent for tribute.* What Mr. Wells and Mr. Fargo saved on way-station horses they spent to discourage predators. He couldn't see any fault in the practice, so long as he himself continued to deliver on it. In its way it was a testament to his efficiency, as well as a guarantor of his dismissal should he fail to live up to his reputation. A man is only as good as his most recent success.

Better and better. He'd feared growing roots in his present position.

Still and all, he thought—excavating Bart's snatch of doggerel from the disorganized (or so it seemed to the uninitiated observer) rubble on his desk—the fellow promised to deliver him from the run-of-the-mill chase. He could scarcely blame the sensation-mongering press for seizing on such dash when it was allowed to fall into their hands; it smacked of Dick Turpin and the Penny Dreadful, and thousands in circulation. Almost by the week, Hume spent his wits on sloths too overcome by inertia to draw wages in the accepted manner, and too feeble-minded to keep themselves to themselves when the deed was done; dulling his well-honed senses as he plodded along the tracks they left, as obvious as those laid down by the Union Pacific.

They led, like as not, to a bathhouse on Pacific Street or a filthy divan in Chinatown, and a fugitive too stupefied on whiskey and opium to make a fight of his capture. Most investigations started in those places and ended there. Trust a bloodhound like Ben Thorn to make a beeline in that direction.

Well, give him that, and spare Hume that particular drudgery. Let a bloodhound like Thorn lust after barroom braggarts to do half his job for him, impressing lewd women with the details of their exploits and broadcasting greenbacks like wheatseed; the sooner he had them by the ear, the sooner he got back to his thirteen rooms, his grand piano, his spoiled wife, and his pack of overprivileged brats, feet propped up on his gout stool and a tanker of English Port in his fist; or whatever was his quaff of choice. For James B. Hume, a greyhound trained to track wolves, a cold supper and a flat belly were his reward and also his tools.

He was born in the Catskill Mountains of New York State, a wild country then, as gaunt and untamed as Oregon before the migration. He'd farmed there and in Indiana, prospected in California, and served as sheriff in that same gold country, where a man's life was sold for as little as a few dollars' worth of dust in his poke. He'd learned that frontier justice was as rough as represented by the eastern press, with gaps like those in a corn rick: A coroner's jury could consider the case of a man shot from behind and assign cause of death to a mishap, because he should have known better than to turn his back on his killer.

Hume would have none of that in his jurisdiction. He'd sent to the state capital in Sacramento for up-to-date penal codes, studied them in the light of tallow candles in reeking tents and by greasy daylight in wayfarers' inns, until he'd learned enough to pass the bar and plead before the bench—if he'd care to take that route.

Which he didn't. Some men are born to bloviate in dusty courtrooms, others to hunt other men. He held no animosity toward lawyers, by and large, but he'd testified in too many trials to pin his hopes on whether the man on the bench approved of his taste in collars; one judge had actually found an attorney in contempt for the color of his cravat. A case built on rock—heelprints, dependable eyewitnesses, and possession of incriminating contraband—trumped the prejudices of the most pettifogging political appointment.

In his capacity as an elected peace officer he'd brought a string of criminal careers to an abrupt end; which was how he'd come to the attention of a beleaguered Wells, Fargo, and eventually to their employ.

It was soon after his recruitment that James B. Hume engraved his name in Company legend. Over and above the strenuous objections of Henry Wells and William Fargo, the detective chief commissioned a headstone to be erected over a bandit slain during an attempted holdup of a Company stagecoach, with an epitaph that afterward became part of frontier lore. Steeply engraved into the limestone, it read:

WELLS, FARGO NEVER FORGETS

He himself was vague on the details of the event. He'd been asked about it so many times it was possible he'd come to accept a myth as fact. But it sounded like something he might have done, so he let the story stand, without either confirming it or denying it. In the end, it served the same purpose as a genuine stone.

"No, Mr. Black Bart," he said, letting a mouthful of cigar smoke drift thick as cream from between his lips toward his tobacco-stained ceiling, "I don't intend to forget you."

# FIVE

*Bart liked the high life the Golden Gate had:*
*music, fandangos, and roe of the shad.*
*'Twasn't his fault to enjoy such delights*
*he had to keep Jim Hume from sleeping at night.*

I n the scarlet history of frontier justice, James B. Hume's method of tracking desperadoes was hardly material for *Ned Buntline's Own* or *Frank Leslie's Illustrated Newspaper*, with their breathless accounts of ambidextrous gunplay, midnight rides, and sudden sweeps of fire and steel, accompanied by Goyesque images inked in blood and pressed on brimstone, to quicken the hearts of passersby and separate them from their nickels. Files, not six-guns, were his weapons of choice. The cabinets containing this armory formed twin rows eight feet high and a block long, leading from the front entrance to the rear exit of the Company's Montgomery Street headquarters, broken only by lath-and-plaster partitions erected between offices. By daylight and coal oil Hume pored over typeface and pencil scrawl, burning cigars by the box, so that a century later the thumb-stained onionskin sheets still yielded the rich, peaty odor of the blend of tobacco he shared with President Grant. Sometimes in person, more often with the cooperation of local peace officers and citizens' committees of vigilance, he collected details—an apple core here, a broken match there, and rung by rung assembled a ladder that would inexorably lead to arrest and punishment.

Wells, Fargo never forgets.

But having begun to form a definite opinion of Black Bart's likes and dislikes based on the evidence, he would have been chagrinned to learn that his quarry enjoyed the look, sound, and smell of well-bred horses racing one another round a track. Had the detective known this at the early gathering stage of the manhunt, he might have assigned something other than prejudice to the man's insistence on traveling afoot. He would not have ruled out broadening the investigation to include spectators at racing events, and possibly have brought the saga of Black Bart to a close much sooner and with less embarrassment to the Company.

Side-by-side with the fighting ring, Ocean View Park was Bolton's venue of choice: The powerful, egg-shaped muscles rolling under sleek coats, the explosive snorts of breath spent on the stroke with pounding hooves, the intoxicating blend of clean sharp sweat, fresh manure, and salt breeze from the Pacific tinged with fish, brought a physical reaction to his testicles he found otherwise only at ringside and in the act of love. Together with the crisp rustle of paper and green-ink smell as he exchanged banknotes for cardboard tickets at the bettors' window, the sensuous image was as close to complete as anything he'd experienced in the curtained balconies in the Bella Union, emblematic of the Barbary Coast.

He had no special dislike for horses as transportation. He merely eschewed the business of saddling and straddling one of the beasts on his excursions after Wells, Fargo gold; swift as they were, they left prints as indelible as Bertillon measurements of ears, noses, chins, and the space between the eyes that the Pinkerton National Detective Agency had employed to identify known miscreants; and in the West, where men's faces were less noted than the set and gait of a particular horse, one's transportation of choice was as damning as an indiscreet boast whispered into the ear of a lady hostess in Portsmouth Square. Bootprints, as shallow as a man's own weight and as anonymous as a thousand pairs of ready-made soles, were no more traceable than clippings on the floor of a barbershop.

But give Charles E. Bolton a small man aboard a muscular specimen of horseflesh, ten dollars of William Wells and Henry Fargo's money on how they finished, and he was as happy as Adam before the Fall, win or lose.

He placed, as it turned out; on Lee's Choice in the third. New Yorker that he was, he held a sentimental sympathy for such lost causes as the Confederacy; and for that matter with the rebels and brigands of history, harkening back to Robin Hood and the Thief on the Cross. For all his disapproval of Jesse James's brand of brutal outlawry, Bolton owned that the man had put his guerrilla experience to work chivvying Big Railroad, whose barons were the latest in a long line of desk-bound pirates who preyed on the independent without so much as drawing a gun and placing themselves at risk.

The clerk at the window, recognizing him, smiled. "You've the luck of the Irish, sir, and no mistake."

Bolton noted the young man's red hair and fair skin. "You must take care not to let it rub off on strangers. There may come the day when you'll need it in a time of urgency."

"Bless you." The clerk exchanged the customer's ticket for twenty-five dollars in gold notes; backed, to Bolton's intense satisfaction, by Wells, Fargo, & Co. of San Francisco.

Hume, brooding before his open window, pressed the efficient Jon Thacker to maintain a close watch on sudden spenders in the region, particularly in the wake of each assault upon a Company stage. "These fellows are not in it for a comfortable retirement. Easy come, easy go, and the easier it comes the swifter it goes."

"In San Francisco, sir?"

"In San Francisco, and what of it?"

"Nothing, sir."

In his wake, Hume lamented the man's lack of gumption in the presence of a superior. Anyone could see the fallacy of his course of action in that city, where honest money evaporated at the same rate as ill-gotten gains. But better to keep his staff alert and their minds on Black Bart, rather than cede the initiative to an unpredictable brigand on his field of choice. Waiting was both the detective's best weapon and his worst enemy.

*　*　*

"What is your secret, if I may be so bold?"

Bolton frowned at the woman who'd spoken, from third

place in line at the bettors' window at Ocean View; for he certainly thought the query bordering on brazen. But his countenance relaxed in the presence of a comely—if comfortably upholstered—lady of ripe years decked out in yards of brocade with an aviary of plumes nested in the curled brim of a hat mounted at an angle he found insolent; but a man who subsidized his pleasures at gunpoint was not necessarily put off by such airs. She was accompanied by a mousy woman half her age, in a gray cotton dress and a plain straw hat and under it the face of a sheep.

"A youth dogged by misfortune," said he in response to her question, tipping his bowler. "I seem to be making up for it in my crepuscular old age."

"Not so decrepit as that, certainly. However, if your sunnier years have manufactured what is vulgarly referred to as a 'hunch'—?" Her smile was white, and quite obviously porcelain.

He turned her aside and whispered the name of a horse that had an admirable history of performance on a muddy track, and since a drizzle had commenced ten minutes before, confided she might do worse than two dollars.

No stranger, she, to a "hunch," as she demonstrated by ceding her place to the person behind her and approaching the ten-dollar window, where no one was waiting.

Bright's Dream paid off at five to one, and thus began a friendship.

She was the forty-seven-year-old widow of a tinpan miner who'd expired of alcohol poisoning in a tent saloon called (ironic though it may seem, but appropriate if one knew the miners' parlance of the time) the Dry Place. "He was a bibulous man," the widow professed, "wanting in every refinement: But, oh, my!" And—on the gospel—she fanned herself. She seemed to have stepped directly from the pages of Jane Austen, cheerfully unaware of the irony intended by the author; yet he found her company entertaining, if only for the giddy joy of anticipating the next gust of confidence on her part, and the exposure connected.

They saw what was almost certainly the thousand-and-first American performance of *East Lynn* at the Metropolitan Theatre, partook of pâté and the *filet de boeuf* in the dining room of the Palace Hotel, and attended *Fra Diavalo* at the Grand Opera House; always with the ovine companion—a hired convenience, as it turned out—in tow. Bolton, who kept a running account of his finances, marveled at the accelerated rate of their decline under certain social circumstances, particularly with the extra baggage factored in; should this whirlwind continue, another withdrawal from the bank of Wells and Fargo would soon be necessary.

"Isn't that Governor Stanford?"

The trio was descending one of the pair of staircases that swept to the opera house's tiled lobby, lock-stepping along with the throng in evening dress eager for refreshment, discourse, and a smoke during intermission. Near the base of the stairs opposite moved a tall, heavy, immaculately bearded man of about Bolton's age, one hand gripping a gold-knobbed stick similar to his own, his thick neck reddening where it met his stiff butterfly collar. On his arm was a plump pink woman, presumably his wife, girdled with diamonds.

"Yes, that is he." Bolton slowed a bit more, allowing the former mining-supply merchant, Central Pacific Railroad president, and Republican governor of California sufficient time to lose himself in the crowd. This spared him an awkward excuse. Although he knew Stanford and his set well enough to pass a few words in greeting, he avoided further colloquy with those familiar enough with the details of harvesting gold to catch "mining speculator" Bolton in a blunder.

Two days later, during his ritual dinner with cattleman Matt Leacock and whaling magnate Alec Fitzhugh, he turned the conversation away from his windfall at the track (everyone, it seemed, was convinced he'd stumbled upon a foolproof wagering system, or was somehow privy to inside intelligence) toward *Fra Diavalo*: "You have seen it, of course?"

"Wild horses couldn't drag me." Leacock's broad face was flushed. The milk-to-brandy ratio in his goblet had tipped in favor of the latter. "I understand that in your case it took only two fillies to manage the thing."

Bolton kept his expression even; inwardly condemning Nob Hill's network of spies to scandalmongers' hell. "Friends, who share an interest in music."

"Liszt, no doubt?" Fitzhugh's leer was in keeping with his table manners; his watch chain had dipped into his chowder not once but twice in the course of the meal. The Hungarian composer's airs were rumored to excite unladylike passions in his female listeners.

Bolton found the drift of the exchange becoming distasteful. He wondered what it said about a man that he considered his friends tiresome.

That had not always been the case; but those had been associations of an entirely different sort. Sometimes he wished—but, no; he had long ago cut loose his team from the wagon of Regret and hitched it to Action.

"Come, come, fellows. I'm past all that."

But his companions were not. Leacock, who was anything but ungenerous with his hoard of rumor, filled him in on the popular history of his Ocean View Park acquaintance. Her late husband, it was suspected, had succumbed to the Demon before he got round to filing a claim on his bonanza. A miners' court held that his signature on a late-found document in Sacramento was valid, and his heirs assured.

"There you have it," said Bolton. "However do these things get started?"

"Possibly it's because every other bit of paper endorsed by the dead man bore an *X* instead of a full signature."

"A man can learn to read and write."

"Perhaps. I should think busting rocks from first light to moonrise on hardtack and water would leave a fellow too broke down for books and schoolwork. But you know the life, and I do not."

Providentially, their waiter arrived to refill Bolton's water glass, providing him the opportunity to change the subject; but he was troubled by Leacock's revelation, and in solitude returned to it from time to time.

He considered taking money face-to-face with an empty gun in wild country a more straightforward enterprise than doing it with a full pen in a parlor; but the woman was comely, if a bit hefty from the rich San Francisco cuisine, and generous with female pheromones. He continued the relationship, escorting her to museums, galleries, and other entertainments, chaperoned by her companion; and when the time came for him to slip the key to his quarters under the table in the little tea room off the foyer of the Webb House, it was the companion who transferred it to her reticule and climbed the back stairs to his floor.

# SIX

*The hound and the fox, they are rarely at peace;*
*one chasing, one fleeing, will they ever surcease?*
*Yet would they stop running, and examine their place,*
*they might see they're each just a dog in the race.*

I s this the item you've been expecting, sir?"

The postal clerk laid the parcel, wrapped in brown paper and bound with cord, on the counter. He was a doughy man in his twenties whose cravat would not be restrained by the bib of his apron, a chronic disorder and a source of mild nuisance to Bolton, who forbore to remark upon it.

The customer examined the package, plastered with stamps and bearing a Chicago postmark. "It is indeed." He thanked the young man and touched the brim of his bowler.

A man who left nothing to chance, he took the bundle back to his room before opening it and trying on the contents, standing on the throw rug to avoid scratching the soles on bare floor, should the fit prove inadequate and require returning. When he lifted the cover from the pasteboard box, a puff of new leather came out; not quite as inebriating as ground grain in a sack-turned-mask, but pleasing as fresh-ground coffee beans.

Fastidiously, he transferred the protective nest of excelsior—shredded remnants of pages from the Montgomery Ward catalogue—to the trash basket, removed wads of *Chicago Sun* from the toes of the boots nestled yin-yang fashion inside the box, and inspected each. They were a somewhat disconcerting shade of yellow, offending both his sense of gentlemanly dress and his fears of easy identification; but the dust of the road would take care of that. The soles were reassuringly thick, the V-shaped elastic inserts on the inside of the shanks pliable. He tugged them on with little resistance, stood, and stamped his heels inside. They slipped a little when he walked in them, but that was good; his old feet had suffered enough from too-close contact with stiff animal hide over long distances. He circled the room, leaving the shelter of the rug, and approved.

The true test was still a way off. When the arrangement the widow (and the paid companion) ended with her decision to trade northern California's fog and damp for a season in Denver, the expense of entertaining gentle company departed with them, and he discovered that his cash reserves would support his quiet masculine lifestyle through the following spring and, if he forewent the races and fights, a month of summer.

This decision was precipitated less by common frugality than caution. He read with interest an editorial in the *Union* of Yreka, California:

> We learn the Shasta and Redding Stage was stopped
> on Thursday morning near Shasta by highwaymen

and compelled to give up the Wells, Fargo Company's express. . . . This makes the third time within a
week that highwaymen have stopped the stage within
Shasta County and the fourth time within two weeks.
This is getting somewhat monotonous for the people
of Shasta County and we expect to hear about the
next thing, that some highwaymen have been seri-
ously hurt. . . .

If the publisher of a journal, whose livelihood was founded
on subscriptions, was growing weary of road agentry, then
so were his readers. That a shipment should be waylaid was
no longer just a possibility, but an event to be taken for
granted. This was a perception the Company could not afford to be broadcast. Bolton placed no credence in the editor's suggestion that Washington be petitioned to supply an
escort of U.S. Cavalry to a civilian enterprise—it had stead-
fastly resisted every call to interfere in domestic matters
since the bad old days of vigilantism—but arms were inevitable. Black Bart had been scrupulous to avoid encounters
with trained shotgun messengers by preying upon modest
shipments, but the zealotry of his competitors might inspire
additional recruitment and deployment across the board.
Patience was the soul of discretion, and he was confident
that Wells and Fargo's native parsimony would reassert itself
once the cost of prevention outdistanced that of plunder.
Give them some victories, or a lengthy dry spell while the
red ink mounted and the black ink remained static, and the
hired guns would be seeking other employment.

Meanwhile, Black Bart would take a piece of his retirement the way most pensioners did, by dining simply, doling

out his pleasures, and counting pennies. He returned the marvelous new boots to their box and placed it behind his collection of bowlers on the top shelf of the wardrobe, humming to himself.

> *Oh, there was Major Thompson, turned up the*
> *other day.*
> *He said he would hold 'em up or the devil'd be*
> *to pay.*
> *For he could hold a rifle and draw a bead so fine*
> *on those shotgun messengers of the Wells, Fargo*
> *line.*

Jim Hume, who ordinarily drew fuel from the din of Montgomery Street, shut his windows against a drunk singing "The Wells, Fargo Line" as he passed the building. The tune was getting to be as popular as "Sweet Betsy from Pike," but a damn sight more irritating; the fellow could not be unaware of his audience. The day was coming when Black Bart would command a quatrain of his own.

Meanwhile Hume took bittersweet solace from the death of a "flour sack bandit" at the hands of a fearless Company messenger whose ten-gauge shotgun had taken off both the man's mask and his head on the Redding run at four o'clock on a frosty morning in December. A hastily convened posse had tracked his two companions to a bed of pine needles, where they were engaged in sleeping off a celebratory drunk, using stolen mail sacks for pillows. The report of the slain badman quickened the detective's heart, but he was disillusioned to learn that the stage's lead horse had been slain in the first round of gunfire at the scene of the robbery.

Although he clung to his belief that Black Bart held the animal in contempt, his behavior on four previous occasions predisposed him against violence directed at man or beast. Plainly, Bart's preferred method of disguise had been preempted by an admirer. If, God forbid, Bart's predilection toward poetasty became general knowledge, Robbers Roost would be paved with couplets, sonnets, and dithyrambs, and the publisher of the *Yreka Union* would forget his jade and engage James Russell Lowell to edit.

Apart from the satisfaction of having checked three predators off the Company's roster, Hume took little comfort from the capture of a trio of blundering comic-opera scoundrels; he flattered himself he could have done the thing himself by way of Western Union, without leaving his desk, and anticipated no more than a paragraph in the columns to commemorate the affair, what with range wars in New Mexico, silver-strike fury in Arizona, and Jesse James sightings everywhere burning out presses across the continent. He wanted this Black Bart, for no especial reason apart from the challenge. *Then* let the rapscallions of the press make what they want of the thief's idiosyncrasies. Not for Hume's own aggrandizement; certainly not for that. He cared not a whit for the glory the association might bring; truth to tell, he disliked seeing his name in print, and wholeheartedly detested being called upon to discuss the details of his own activities on behalf of his employers. As well ask a dry-goods merchant how many overalls he'd sold; what did it signify, so long as he was still in business at the end of the year? A man could afford to be magnanimous in victory, that was all.

So the two men sat in their respective lairs—literally

around the corner from each other; they had more than once passed on the street, without so much as noticing another stranger among the hundreds who swelled the population daily. One man faced east, the other west, their profiles beak-nosed and high-browed, like obverse sides of a two-headed coin; neither knowing how much he resembled the other: seeker and sought, in a tale that might have been told by Poe, in which one destroyed his double, and in the act destroyed himself. Neither knew how closely their lives matched. Hume, like Bolton, enjoyed laying wagers on contests of skill and speed; both took pride in keeping meticulous records, the bandit of his finances, the detective of his investigations. They preferred a four-in-hand knot over the half-hitch; crossed their t's with a bold stroke, forming a dog-trot roof across most of the word; each had been reared in rural New York State, a continent and also a world away from bawdy San Francisco, two years apart, and moved to the Midwest to farm. Both had arrived in the gold fields in the fall of 1850, and met with scant success. It was not impossible that they had drunk ice-cold water from the same stream, passed each other on the way to and from their claims, and staked them in Sacramento within days of each other.

In 1877, James B. Hume knew nothing about Black Bart except the vague (and oftentimes contrary) descriptions left by confused passengers and defensive drivers, his devious dressing-up of his robbery sites, his courtly conceit when demanding his booty (as if "please" gave the drivers the option of refusal), the Calvary-cross shape left by his knife upon slashing open a mail sack, his shotgun (never fired, even to instill fear), his soiled duster, his "Ku-Kluxer" head-

mask, his hatchet, and his singular method of transportation for a criminal undertaking, which generally depended
on the briefest of confrontations followed by the swiftest
possible exit, commonly aboard a reliable horse; this one depended on his feet. The detective placed his faith in the
duster and flour sack, the hatchet and the gun, the tools of
Bart's trade—things the witnesses all seemed to agree
upon—and his bootprints in the dirt, unaccompanied by
the marks of shod hooves. The scrap of doggerel he'd left at
the scene of his latest atrocity was frosting only, but volatile
stuff should it fall into the laps of the accursed journalists.
It was just the sort of shiny detritus they fell upon, like crows
on foil.

Charles E. Bolton knew even less about his adversary—
nothing, in fact, owing to Hume's abhorrence of notoriety. His name had not yet appeared in the newspapers in
connection with the case. That would not be the situation
much longer, thanks to the insatiable appetite of the carrion-
birds of the press.

How Hume loathed them; their filthy bowlers, yellow
collars, tattered topcoats, shrill, overlapping queries, and
constant scribbling in their writing-blocks, picking over the
juiciest morsels left to rot in the sun, reeking and aswarm
with flies, to serve them up to their eager readers like the
pheasants the Palace Hotel imported from England, packed
in dry ice and roasted to a golden turn. A brigand in California, a railroad magnate caught with his thumb in the
till, a ship lost in the Atlantic, preferably packed with dead
passengers; they throve on disaster.

Down in the street, the drunk had resumed his taunt,
the rise and fall of his atrocious chant penetrating window

and shutters. But no, Hume reasoned, as he flung up the sash to rid the room of its tobacco fog, and heard only the usual clatter and bang from the pavement below; it was just his imagination run riot. The double panes had snuffed out most of the cacophony of the calamitous city, and the bothersome brute had long since migrated to the next gin-house, to spread his poisonous rhyme throughout the establishment. The blasted air had tunneled its way into Hume's brain like a burrowing insect, playing over and again, like a hurdy-gurdy on Pacific Street grinding out its wheezy refrain. It was one of those ditties, which, like "Sweet Betsy from Pike," took on a new stanza with each listener; and each chorus a nail in Hume's coffin with Mr. Valentine, the superintendent, and a most impatient man, who knew nothing at all of the quiet perseverance required of the hunt. Popular music-hall fare had a permanence that history itself, and human memory, lacked; give an event the proper blend of horror and romance, add in rhythm and lilt, and it became as much a part of vulgar culture as Johnny Appleseed and Guy Fawkes. A detective was only as good as his most recent arrest, just as a bandit was only as good as his most recent robbery; and a man as clever as Black Bart, who with nothing more than a handful of sticks had worked out the problem of acting alone—thus eliminating the danger of betrayal by a loquacious accomplice— might go on stinging the Company long after his pursuer had lost his place.

The chief of detectives, who prided himself upon the scientific process, eschewing emotion, could not know that by the following August, the game he'd entered into would turn into something more personal than any of the others, and that in addition to Bart's mere apprehension he would long to mount his head on his office wall, stuffed with sawdust and with a plaque underneath reading:

WELLS, FARGO NEVER FORGETS

Perhaps that would drive the troublesome tune out of his skull.

# SEVEN

*Now, the fox seldom sees the face of the hound;*
*when the dog bays, he scurries to get underground.*
*But Bart got a look at his hunter by chance;*
*it was then they went into the highwayman's dance.*

D ail Callahan had emigrated from county Kilkenny
with his parents to San Francisco a year after the first
color surfaced at Sutter's Mill, father Fergus having
sold his plows, sacks of manure, and stacked Surcoat brand
overalls, along with his shop, to pay for steamship passage
and outfit himself for prospecting.

He found no gold; at least not in its raw state.

"Come too late to the ball," he told those who asked.

Disdaining to tot up his losses, he'd followed the lead of
visionaries who'd spun dross into dollars by unloading their
equipment to fellow hopefuls at a steep profit and investing
the proceeds in other enterprises. He established a dry-goods
store on Mission Street, in a building then under construction on the site of a Chinese laundry burned out by Denis
Kearney's vigilantes.

It was a generation before the Callahans found themselves

in circumstances superior to those they'd left behind. Dail, Fergus' principal heir, now supplied his customers with all their daily necessaries, including picks and shovels, cultivators, cloth goods, ladies' Parisienne hats, bone china, Pears soap, licorice twists, stem-winders in gold, silver, and pewter, Kidney-Wort, hair restorers for men and women, a brass Babcock fire extinguisher the size of a fireplug, and a fine array of firearms ("The best selection west of Denver") and boxes of ammunition stacked ten feet high on shelves behind the counter, graduating from light birdshot at waist level past Smokeless Sporting Rifle and Military Cartridges to buffalo rounds accessible only by ladder or with the handy tool he'd inherited from his father, with a clamp on one end connected by a spring to a trigger on the other.

Pressed for details, Callahan allowed as how no one had actually come in to purchase the heavier artillery since the big shaggies had been hunted clean out of existence. However, he ceded the valuable space it took up because the oblong crate and its ominously stenciled DANGER—HIGH EXPLOSIVES furnished a topic of conversation that frequently led to a transaction, especially among pilgrims conditioned by spectacular accounts of Russian imperial bison hunts and sharpshooting exploits by homegrown frontiersmen of the Bill Cody sort, inflated sufficiently to bring a flush to the cheeks of Natty Bumppo. The longer a curious party remained in conversation, the more likely the sale.

For himself, the proprietor wasn't any great shakes as a "conversator," claiming not only that he'd never kissed the Blarney Stone, but he'd not heard it so much as mentioned until he came to America; "nor leprechauns nor shamrocks neither, come to that," he'd added, for he prided himself

upon his Presbyterian practicality as opposed to Dublinesque
Roman Catholic mysticism. Apart from that subject—which
came up whenever a customer commented on his tacitur-
nity—he let others discover the stout container on the top
shelf with its Pandora's-box warning and ask what it contained. Then he would affirm that the caliber and manufacturer had been endorsed in advertisements by none other
than Buffalo Bill, he of the Wild West exhibition, and did
nothing to discourage assumptions that the famed fron-
tiersman was a frequent patron. He'd found exploiting a
Yankee mythology more beneficial to his commercial interests than sprites and four-leaf clovers.

"I'm not interested in that eyewash," Jim Hume told the
merchant, barely into his account of the Battle at Warbon-
net Creek. In truth the detective chief's gaze had wandered
ceilingward only because it was his custom upon entering
any public place to look all about him. "This is what I came
in for." He produced a cigar-shaped object from a pocket
and placed it on the counter.

Callahan looked at it without picking it up. It was made
of stiff paper, hollow and faded red, with a brass ferrule,
pitted by weather, and the manufacturer's name stenciled on
the paper. Finally he took it between thumb and forefinger
and sniffed at the open end, his nose wrinkling away from
burnt sulfur and saltpeter. He turned it to peer at the stamping on the flanged metal end, confirming what he'd already
determined. He put it down.

"Ten-gauge buck," he reported, in the lilt he'd brought
over at age sixteen and brushed up in Corktown every Saturday night.

"I know. I'm asking if you can identify it."

"To what end?"

Hume took out his commission papers and his badge, shield-shaped pewter with WELLS, FARGO, & CO. engraved in arching letters on the top third and DETECTIVE across the center. It irked him that the dry-goods man gave only cursory reference to the former and concentrated on the latter. The papers were signed by the partners who'd founded the firm and notarized by a legal secretary in the governor's office in Sacramento. The embossed seal alone was more difficult to counterfeit than a scrap of metal.

"Is it Black Bart?"

Hume felt his face darken another shade. Despite all the measures he'd taken to maintain the bandit's anonymity outside his office, the name was too melodramatic to remain in-house. How soon before street talk made it into print, and Bart's verse leapt into the lead column? His jabbery staff was in for a thunderous shaking-out.

From another pocket he drew a drawstring bag and spilled out its contents next to the shotgun shell. There were sixteen, each the size of a cherry pit and made of blackened lead. Some were squashed and flattened by contact with cartilage and bone, but most retained their original spherical shape.

"A sheriff's posse dug them out of a horse slain on the Redding road. That shell was found at the scene."

"It's buckshot, sure enough. Whether these came from that—"The shopkeeper pointed from the leaden pellets to the paper tube. He rolled a beefy shoulder.

Hume had come away from the office with his pockets sagging. He held up another shell similar to the first, except the end opposite the ferrule was crimped and sealed, heavy with shot, the brass shone bright yellow, and the red dye was as vivid as the pip on the ace of hearts. The same information was stenciled on the paper. "We confiscated this from a man currently in custody." He broke it in half egg-fashion and dumped the unfired shot like coriander seeds beside the spent rounds. Some of them rolled off the edge of the surface and tap-tap-tapped on the cedar plank floor.

Callahan retrieved a square of slate-colored emory cloth from a shelf under the counter. He dropped a piece of the spent shot onto it, rubbed it vigorously inside the cloth, separated it, and examined it in the strong sunlight coming through the plate-glass window facing the street. He grunted, then picked up one of the shiny bits from the fresh shell, but this time he didn't use the cloth. He held it up and compared it to the shot recovered from the slain horse; grunted again.

"I sell this kind. The manufacturer alloys the lead with copper; see it shine like gold when it's new, and the same when it's old and you polish it. Lead's soft, butchering the flesh it hits; but the copper, being harder, bounces off bone and makes more mischief as it strays off course. That's the story they give me to tell, and excuse the price."

"A moment ago you weren't so certain you could match it."

"I wasn't sure how far you intended to take the matter. A man has to protect his customers. What difference does one horse more or less make to me?"

"A man died as well. A load of shot like this one blew open his head like a melon. I would just as soon hang a man for keeping his mouth shut as for pulling the trigger on another. What difference does one storekeep more or less make to me?"

The Irishman's face didn't change. His father had been the first to break away from a long line of tenant farmers schooled by generations of behavior to refuse lord and Mother Nature the satisfaction of showing displeasure at their treatment; misery expressed led only to more torment. "I'm not the only one in town carries it."

"The others said the same thing. They all kept records of the people they sold it to."

Callahan grunted a third time and hoisted his account book onto the counter.

Hume came away with his evidence, but in a sourer mood than when he'd stepped into the shop. Snaring the wretches with their muzzy heads brazenly resting on stolen mail sacks had been enough to deny them their freedom; matching the buckshot to its purchasers merely gave the judge less of an excuse to turn them back into public congress earlier. It was running in place, is what it was, and scarcely a deterrent to others who would quite naturally consider themselves too clever to stumble so easily into capture. There were times when the job seemed less a matter of fighting crime than keeping a record of it. Bart, especially, would smirk; he'd already proven to belong to a different species from the garden-variety bush-ranger. Such as they who preyed on the Redding stage were men "the Po8" would not allow to lace his well-worn boots.

But, happier thought: Did Hume really wish for his man to take alarm and leave off pillaging entirely, never to be heard from in this life? That would be as unsatisfactory as tossing a feather down a well and waiting forever to hear the splash. Let the fellow grow bolder and bolder yet, and stack brick upon reckless brick until the structure collapsed out from under him. And God willing and the Company didn't sack him, Hume would be waiting at the base holding a net.

Against his predictions—and, considering the result, to his intense displeasure—the Yreka-Redding stage robbery would *not* be buried on the inside pages of the *Examiner* and the *Bee* among the testimonials for St. Jacob's Oil and genuine marble monuments. Instead it had the effect of catapulting Wells, Fargo, & Company's chief of detectives into public notice. His scientific method of narrowing down the supplier of the bandits' ammunition (for it *was* Dail Callahan, as confirmed by his account book) had added fresh seasoning to the stale subject of stage-road skullduggery, and for the first time the name of James B. Hume appeared prominently in print. It scarcely mattered that the man himself turned away all requests for interviews, and when he could not avoid them dampened their queries with monosyllabic responses (as opposed to driving them off with a stick). The knaves made up what they liked, and no one to catch them at it before the damage was done.

One man who found the items of interest read them in detail in his room in the Webb House, waiting for the steaming water in his basin to soak away the miseries of his feet. At that period in journalism, coarse newsprint would not accept a photograph. But staff artists, working mainly from descriptions supplied by observant reporters ("Mount Vanderbilt's bald dome on R. B. Hayes's face;" "Remove Horace Greeley's eyeglasses and shave off his Mormon's whiskers; that's the fellow"), rendered fair likenesses of persons of celebrity, to be etched into zinc and transferred to the page as faithfully as the ruff round Lydia Pinkham's neck.

Hume's three-quarter profile sprang out at Bolton, causing him nearly to upset the basin in which he was soaking his feet. He thought he'd been found out, so close was the resemblance to himself. The caption steadied his pulse.

He settled himself down to a close study, like a Union general committing to memory the features of his Confederate counterpart, in order to know him from the outside in. He read of the detective's discovery, by scientific method, of the source of a robber band's ammunition; of the long roll of his past successes in bringing criminals to justice; amused himself with the legend of the headstone and the inscription that had since become the Company's credo.

He read to the end of the column, then looked again at the face of his nemesis. The corners of his moustaches twitched upward. "Pleased to make your acquaintance, Mr. Hume."

Thereupon he toweled off, pulled on his stockings, and rose to retrieve his new walking boots from the wardrobe.

It was July 1878; nearly a year since Black Bart had made his last appearance.

# EIGHT

*Poets come in every sort,*
*bad, middling, and terrific;*
*but give them paper, time, and sport,*
*they're apt to be prolific.*

The owner of a walnut grove situated outside Yuba City piloted an elm wagon drawn by four laboring Percherons through the up-and-downest portion of Butte County, bearing a load of logs toward the sawmill at Berry Creek with a Winchester shotgun at his feet, one barrel loaded with salt, the other with Champion double-o buck. Good hardwood was valuable in a country where towns sprang up like thistle, and he little thought bandits in that stretch would scruple against snaring a load of lumber, should they get bored while waiting for a stagecoach.

The horses, stout as they were—their bloodlines stretched back to the armored steeds of medieval jousts—slung strings of lather as they pulled the ponderous load through the summer heat, which despite the thinness of the mountain air was stifling. The bark on the logs drew clouds of gnats that clustered in their nostrils and the corners of their eyes, and deer flies attacked that particular delicacy, the back of a sweating man's neck, to be swatted with a curse, rolled into pellets, and flung aside to make room for the next siege; but his oaths were halfhearted. He was saving the really profane kind for flightless vermin of the two-legged variety. If the sting of the salt didn't discourage them, the lead pellets in the second barrel would settle the matter.

Thus, when he caught the rare sight of a stranger in a soiled linen duster seated on a boulder alongside the road, he leaned closer to the scattergun. They were near enough to the mill to smell the clean sharp scent of fresh-cut wood, and the road itself was paved so heavily with yellow chips it could pass for a slab of longhorn cheese.

The pilgrim looked up from the square of foolscap he was writing on with a thick carpenter's pencil, touched the brim of an incongruous bowler hat, and returned to his scribbles. On the ground beside the boulder lay a bedroll, the blanket faded from its original red-and-black check to a dirty pink under a skin of dust. From the look of its lumpy contours, the lumberman assumed it contained all of the fellow's possessions, and assigned to him the somewhat more common character in those parlous times of a vagabond drifting from one odd job to another. He straightened in his seat, leaving the weapon on the footboard. True, many of these tramps were far less inoffensive than popular lore painted them; but this one's whiskers were tipped with gray, and his sagging features and the defeated slope of his shoulders made him more worthy of pity than fear. Certainly he made no move toward whatever was in his bundle. The scrap of paper braced on his thigh commanded all his attention. Had the light not been fleeting, and the grove owner in a more Christian mood, he might have tossed a handful of coppers the fellow's way.

When, two hours later, he finished helping to unload in Berry Creek and the sawmill operator rubbed his hands at the quality of the delivery and estimated the profit to them both, he felt bad that he hadn't been charitable; but the wastrel was gone by the time he headed back home along the same road.

Instead the man was asleep, swaddled in his blanket in a cedar copse fifty yards off, resting in preparation for a busy day beginning in the morning. Beside him lay his abbreviated shotgun, and in a pocket of his overalls was folded the piece of paper he'd been writing on earlier. The legend ran:

> *Here I lay me down to sleep,*
> *to wait the coming morrow.*
> *Perhaps success, perhaps defeat,*
> *and everlasting sorrow.*
> *Let come what will I'll try it on,*
> *my condition can't be worse;*
> *and if there's money in that box*
> *'tis munny in my purse.*

> —Black Bart, the Po8.

\* \* \*

"Blast and damn!"

The curse was vehement, but not loud. After all, a man who persisted in working with his windows open to a busy street could not afford to be overheard spitting blasphemies like a drunken oaf in Sydneytown.

It was not commonly known, but Wells and Fargo placed only second behind the Pinkerton National Detective Agency in the employment of spies. Its operatives and informants burrowed deep into locations where they were least expected—not only in criminal gangs, silently recording the illegal enterprises in which they themselves performed as accomplices, but even in law enforcement, where they enforced the statutes they were appointed or elected to defend while furnishing regular reports to Jim Hume regarding persons and events exclusively of interest to the Company. One of these sub rosa agents, a paid-up member of the Printers Guild, had toiled for years in the press room at the *Eureka*, a San Francisco newspaper with a mammoth circulation.

"Is it extravagant?" John Valentine had complained. "Intelligence from lawmen and outlaws is one thing, prevaricating journalists another. To what gain? An hour's start on every farm wife and harness maker with two coppers in his pocket?"

"And on the thieves who scavenge our shipments, don't forget," Hume had replied. "A good horse moving at a brisk canter travels ten miles in sixty minutes, trailing men who don't know what we know, and so are advancing at an easy walk."

"Evidently, you and I are acquainted with an entirely different breed of horse."

Hume stepped around this disgruntled reference to the superintendent's own experiences betting in Ocean View Park. "In any event, printers are not journalists. It's an honest trade."

Valentine, a man without imagination, but an able administrator, who spent Company money as if it came from his own purse, could be brought round, had one but the endurance to wait out the snail's pace of his reasoning process. The expenditure had been authorized, and here was one result.

Hume studied the sheet the *Eureka* man had brought. Its size, nearly as large as a linen tablecloth, obliged the chief of detectives to rise from behind his desk in order to unfurl and read it.

It represented the front page of that day's number, printed on one side only, and fresh from the screw press used for proofs; some of the ink had smeared in the process of rolling it up and smuggling it out of the shop beneath the printer's knee-length ulster. It bore the newspaper's Old English–style masthead, motto, an advertisement for a wringer-washer, and not one, but *both* of Black Bart's contributions to poesy, set in bold type, the first above the second, in the left column, preceded by an explanatory paragraph under the heading BLACK BART BOLD AS BRASS, and followed by a reasonably accurate accounting of the villain's outrages beginning with Funk Hill in July 1875.

It was somewhat more commonly understood that newspapers, to all intents and purposes, held the patent on domestic espionage. The enemy had penetrated the Company, or at least that group of outsiders it had taken into its confidence. Hume came to this conclusion in the five minutes it took him to read to the end of the column.

He managed to avoid crumpling the expanse of fresh limp paper into an angry ball, folded it unevenly, and asked the man who'd brought it if anyone had seen him enter the building.

"Possibly so, sir; but I told the foreman I had to step out

to cover a draft, and I have a small account with the Company, as you directed. I stashed the sheet under the press table, replaced it, and rolled a fresh proof without anyone knowing what I was about, so they'll never miss this one."

"Don't make a habit of the excuse. Those rogues you work for are liars themselves, and can smell a falsehood under a pile of offal."

When the man had left, Hume bellowed for secretary Thacker, who unfolded the galley sheet and frowned. "They even got the misspelling in the last line."

"More of Bart's chicanery. He got it right the first time. If there's one word he knows how to spell, it's 'money.' Pull the file."

"Which one?"

His superior gave him a wooden-faced look. The man colored and stepped to the drawer containing what they'd gathered on Black Bart. He handed the portfolio to Hume, who jerked loose the tie and rummaged through the familiar contents, coming up at last with the original poems retrieved from the last two robberies, each line written in a different hand. New as the science of calligraphy was, the man was aware of it. He returned them to the pouch and handed it back to Thacker to re-tie and re-file it. The detective was almost disappointed. Proof that evidence had been removed and given to the press would have provided him with the release of turning his staff on the spit, identifying the culprit, and drumming him out.

Here entered a new phase in the history of pillage along the coach roads. What had become tiresome to report was transformed, by a dozen lines of doggerel, into romantic legend. The editors of telegraph columns as far as the

Atlantic coast, their snouts turned continuously into the prevailing winds from the West (where when things happened they happened as suddenly as a boiler bursting), picked up the scent and sprayed it throughout Denver, St. Louis, Chicago, New York City, and Boston, enabling columnists of a literary bent to compare Black Bart to Dick Turpin, Robin Hood, and Spring-heeled Jack.

"Manners, by thunder!" This time, Hume mangled the general-circulation edition into a mass and hurled it into a corner. "Because he says 'if you please' instead of threatening to blow their heads off their shoulders with both barrels aimed straight at them! What has Mrs. Astor to say about that?"

Three hundred seventy-nine dollars in coin had come away with Bart from the Berry Creek road, along with a twenty-five-dollar watch and a diamond ring estimated at two hundred dollars; this tally, at least, remained the exclusive property of Wells and Fargo. Hume found comfort in that, as it indicated his own people were innocent of disloyalty. He'd shared those details with them, but withheld them from the bulletin that had gone out to Company representatives and peace officers; the leaky barrel was not in his building.

But it proved a failure as well. Carving digits off the actual losses—a gambit Hume himself had introduced in order to discourage sensation and turn potential thieves away from the risk—did not in this case repel interest; the hoggish public, and the scalawags who ladled out its slop, were more enchanted by the frilly trimming than the size of the bounty. An account alleging that *Scribner's Monthly* had offered Bart twenty-five dollars against earnings for first serial rights to a book of poetry was denied by the magazine's editor; but not quickly enough to prevent the report from affixing itself permanently to the bandit's mythos; or for that matter before "the Po8" had committed three more robberies—disappointingly failing to add anything new to the slim volume of his verse.

# NINE

*A wolf may grow fat when the pickings are vast,*
*and a man fill his purse when the money comes fast.*
*But this word of warning, to one and to all:*
*In life and in license, pride precedeth a fall.*

The "Sydney Duck"—as locals called the cockney refuse that had washed up from San Francisco Bay after
decades of transportation to Australia for crimes
bad enough to be expelled from England, but not worth
hanging a man over—took note of the fine engraved pocket
watch in the hand of the middle-aged swell waiting in line to
enter the Hippodrome, and wiped his palms on his filthy
trousers so that they wouldn't slip when he employed them.
The fellow looked fair game, straight as a cue-stick in his
sporting outfit, gay but tasteful, with a quiet check, pearl-
gray bowler, and gold-knobbed stick; and when he snapped
shut the lid of the timepiece and tucked it into a waistcoat
pocket at the end of its bright chain, a diamond the size of
a cobblestone refracted green-and-violet light on the ring
finger of his right hand. It was a regular spark-fawney, good
for half a century in the back room of the Devil's Kitchen.

There was frost on the noggin, so he wouldn't put up much of a fight.

That settled the matter, as the duck wasn't a bloke for the fracas; he earned his porridge with his fingers, not his fists. He tugged his cloth cap over his ears so as not to lose it if he had to take it on the ankles, and moved in.

He stopped when the glittery old gent turned to the fellow nearest him and said something that made the man tip back his head and show his uppers. His laughing companion wore the blue tunic, beetle hat, and shield of the city police.

What was a crusher doing attending an illegal prizefight? He ought to be surrounding the building with a dozen of his fellows, awaiting the signal to close in and clear it out.

The old cove was a fly-cop, that was it; posing as a pigeon, flashing merchandise from the evidence room as bait to snare buzz-nappers like the duck. Come to study on it, he looked just like that Wells and Fargo man from the papers.

The longer the duck watched, the more he was sure he'd spared himself a month in the clink. He stuck his dukes deep in his pockets and melted back into the safe crucible of the crowd.

As it happened, the patrolman was under orders not to interfere with the pugilistic exhibition, regardless of the inevitable blowback from Nob Hill's bluenoses; the word was out that Elias J. "Lucky" Baldwin had come all the way up from Los Angeles to take in the fights, and it wouldn't do an officer's career any good to round up the state's biggest speculator along with the mobility. A police presence was required only to see that order was maintained in the event of an upset—and to provide safe passage to the gentry when the rocks and staves came out. Like the pickpocket, he'd spotted the trappings of wealth and approached the gentleman, speaking low:

"Your pardon, sir, but that watch and ring are like catnip in this neighborhood."

The man's pale blue eyes twinkled, bright as his baubles. "Protective coloring, Officer. I thought it better they made off with brass and paste than the notes folded inside my shoe."

The officer tipped back his head, laughed, and strolled away, twirling his baton at the end of its strap. It was good that he was contented with his lot, with no wish for promotion to the detective bureau. The imitations had looked genuine enough for him.

*　*　*

Hiking along the familiar trail, he enjoyed the feel of worn soft wool against his skin, the smell of clean linen when he drew out his handkerchief to mop the back of his neck, the crunch of gravel under his newly broken-in boots, the suffused warmth of Indian summer on his back, like sunshine filtering through a stained-glass window. Peaches hung heavy from their branches, fat and golden as Christmas bulbs. He picked one and bit into it, spilling sticky juice onto his whiskers and obliging himself to lick it from his fingers. Just as middle age—and the first gust from the grave—ripened raw intelligence into refined wisdom, the first frost turned fruit almost achingly sweet, with the bleak awareness behind it of the dead season to come.

Such thoughts caused a man to take stock.

—*Don't know about you, Charlie, but I smell a bonanza.*

—*I do know, Davy. Gold has no odor.*

—*You're too much of a straight thinker. I have formed the conclusion we'll be millionaires in our twenties.*

—*You aim too low, brother. There are better things than being a millionaire.*

—*What are they, I should like to know?*

—*Living like one.*

He looked at his surroundings. Had he and David worked this stretch? The lay bore some resemblance to the North Fork of the American, where they'd scraped up enough for a brief visit back East. It was pretty, unless you wandered far enough off the road to see the gutted earth, the forests clear-cut for cabins, sluices, and timbers, the ground scarred and puckered by unchecked erosion. In any case the brothers had spent too much time chopping and digging and washing silt from their pans, looking for bits of spark, to admire the scenery.

They'd planned to come back and try again, but they never did; not together.

Memories and regrets. They assayed out at a penny a ton, but one could never bring himself to leave them behind.

He neared the settlement of Ukiah, announcing itself, after the nature of all civilization, with trash: empty tins, shattered stays, moldy newspapers, whiskey bottles, and mounds of offal, overhung with soporific flies. He changed course in order to avoid meeting anyone who might remember a stranger traveling on foot. It had been a mistake to let himself be seen the last time, without his hood. If he hadn't been worn out from the hike and afret over his rhyme scheme, he'd have heard the wagon coming and gone to cover. The poetic conceit had gotten to be more trouble than it was worth just to needle the Company. With the town safely behind him he returned to the road, gathered more peaches in his flour sack, tied it to the barrels of his shotgun, rested the stock on his shoulder, and carried the bundle after the fashion of tramps the rest of the way to his preferred vantage point, a great boulder standing sentry by the side of the road with its back to the ocean, that body an invisible presence of salt air and walloping surf beyond pines as tall as grain elevators. He'd come two hundred miles in ten days, had depleted the last of the provisions he'd packed, and caution had prevented him from turning in to a dwelling to seek hospitality. His belly scraped against his ribs, but the peaches kept him from becoming peckish. He stretched his blanket on a bed of fragrant needles, laid out his canteen, hatchet, and shotgun, and sat, eating and tossing the pits, wrinkled like old men's testicles, toward the racket squirrels made hop-scotching through dead maple leaves, loud shuffles a man could mistake for elk.

There came at last a new sound, which as it increased stopped the squirrels in their tracks and stilled the voice of a bullfrog in mid-gulp in an eddy of the Klamath: a traveling symphony made up of creaking leather, joints groaning like tree branches rubbing, the merry tinkle of bit-chains, snorting breaths, and hooves thudding. It was bound south; the Arcata-Ukiah stage, and removing his hat and peeping over the top of his rock, Bart confirmed that no one shared the driver's seat. The mud wagon and its team, shrunken by distance, hauled a plume of rust-colored dust a hundred yards long.

Lowering himself back into cover, he returned his bowler to his head with a dandy's flourish, popped the crown, and shook the rest of the peaches out of his flour sack, whistling under his breath his favorite air.

\* \* \*

"A tall order this time, I'm afraid, Mrs. Yee."

Charles Bolton addressed his laundress in the same politely apologetic tone he applied to coach drivers when asking them to deliver the swag. He placed the bulging canvas drawstring sack the Webb House provided for its preferred guests on the counter with the shame-faced deference of a boy surrendering his pocket catapult to a stern headmaster. Steam drifted through the strings of beads that curtained the doorway opposite him, its damp heat felt rather than seen, laden with the fresh clean scents of cornstarch and warm linen.

But the old Chinese woman was not stern with him. (*How* old she was, none could determine; many of her countrywomen showed faces crumpled like rice paper at the half-century mark; this one, smooth-complected as a young girl under her cap of pulled-back white hair, fine as sugar, gave the impression of having passed that point when she arrived with the first shipment of celestials in 1849.) She sorted through the shirts, collars, stockings, handkerchiefs, and underdrawers. Presently she extracted a stocking and held it aloft, the coarse wool twisted as a root and clotted with spiny seed-cases. She might have been holding up a dead rat by the tail. "You should wear gaiters, Mr. Bo-ton. I can wash and hang out the rest in the time it takes to comb out the cockleburs."

His eyes creased at the corners. Discussing his intimate garments with a woman he scarcely knew was tantamount to conferring with a doctor on the subject of gallstones.

"Gaiters chafe, and are too hot besides. I cover a lot of ground inspecting my claims."

"You are too old to be out hiking. A gentleman who dresses like you can afford to hire someone."

"A lady of your experience should take her own advice. You ought to be rocking and sipping tea on some back porch instead of pressing clothes in a hotbox."

"Who, if not me? My husband and sons left me to work for the railroad and I can trust no one else not to scorch and use too much starch. This, Mr. Bo-ton"—she held up a soiled linen collar—"I should hate to let a fine man like you strangle like a highbinder on the gallows."

"I bow to your wisdom, madam."

And he did.

\* \* \*

The first reports of the holdup near Ukiah were on Hume's desk when a telegram arrived bearing sketchy details of an assault upon the stage from Covelo, the next day along the Potter Valley Road, less than twenty miles away from the first, and bound for the same destination. By now the local authorities were schooled enough in Black Bart's methods to report that empty mail sacks had been found opened with T-shaped slashes in both cases.

"No poem," he muttered.

Sheriff Ben Thorn snorted. "Maybe he's dried up."

"Not where it counts. I can't remember the last time anyone struck two of our coaches inside twenty-four hours."

"They say fortune favors the bold. I've not seen it myself. It leads to carelessness. I expect we'll have him in irons by Christmas."

The detective watched the peacekeeper twirling the platinum crook of his new stick. "I find that observation ironic."

"I don't follow you."

"It wasn't important—to me." He shook his head. "If I were to leave such things to chance, I wouldn't take it against Valentine to give me the sack."

"Perhaps now Bart's laid his pen to rest, the mongrels of the press will move on to other things."

"They won't. They're like badgers once they have their teeth in something."

Thorn left for San Andreas and his palace. Alone in his office, Hume laid out additional evidence from Ukiah: Six peach pits, dry but still ruddy and syrupy sweet to the nose. Bart had scraped his teeth on them; he was that close and yet as far away as ever. Jon Thacker found his employer moving the wrinkled ovals around the yellow Western Union flimsy like chessmen.

"Someone to see you, sir. A lumberman from Yuba City."

"I have no business with a lumberman from Yuba City."

"Perhaps you have with this one. He's come to put in for the reward on Black Bart."

# II

# OUT IN THE WASH

*And what makes robbers bold but too much lenity?*

—William Shakespeare

# TEN

*Bart didn't spring fully growed from a pod;*
*it took many years to make him so odd.*
*Many years and sharp practice made Wells, Fargo rich,*
*and festered and turned Bart's heart blacker than pitch.*

Who was Black Bart?

For that matter, who was Charles Bolton?

His name wasn't Bolton, to begin with. Just why he'd chosen that *nom de société*, no one now knows; especially as it was so close to his own.

Although the press got it right in the end, it could never agree on where Charles E. Boles was born, or the names of his siblings, or for that matter those of his own family, or if he had one. He was the seventh of nine children fathered by John Boles out of Maria Leggett Boles, and in spite of vigorous journalistic attempts to assign him a birth as well as a childhood ironically identical to James B. Hume's on a farm in New York State, records in the local vicarage confirm that he was a British subject, entering the world in 1829 in Norfolk County, England, as was John in 1788.

Charles's youngest sister, Maria, however, had her birth

registered in Jefferson County, New York, in 1832; so he must have arrived in the New World either in swaddling, or in knickerbockers at the outside.

The details of his early life remain shrouded, which is nothing unusual to an upbringing in the country in those years. As far as the history of the man later to be known as Black Bart is concerned, he sprang forth at age twenty in San Francisco in the company of a brother, David, in the watershed year of 1849, sailing thirteen thousand miles through violent storms and stupefying doldrums round Cape Horn in the company of tommies, micks, Scots, French, Prussians, Russians, Poles, Greeks, Basques, Bostoners, fellow New Yorkers, and Philadelphians, all tumescent with the lust for gold. The two arrived seasick, homesick, and frantic to set foot on a surface that didn't roll, pitch, or slant, with what remained of their spirits lashed to splints of banknotes stuffed deep in their stockings—expense money either borrowed or earned by hard labor—and to dreams of returning to New York someday soon, dining and attending entertainments in evening dress, escorting shining women in gems and décolletage, and tipping the fellows who seated them with double eagles.

They found a harbor crowded gunwale-to-gunwale with trim clippers, waddling barges, and ancient tramp steamers, so close together a man could walk two hundred yards to shore without wetting his feet. The city was denser yet, tents and structures built of packing-crates and wrecked seacraft thrown up cheek-by-jowl with no regard for passage between, so that if a greenhorn missed his stop he had to circle the block to resume the quest; certainly the press of traffic behind him—foot, horse, and buckboard—prevented him from reversing directions and walking against the current. It was a reeking pile of rotten potatoes, unscrubbed flesh, last night's slops (and also those of two weeks before), and the occasional corpse, murdered, succumbed to fever, poisoned with wood alcohol sold as whiskey, or starved, turning rancid in the salubrious California climate.

—*Don't know about you, Charlie, but I smell a bonanza.*

David relied overmuch on his snout; their father had whipped him at age three for rooting with the hogs in the pen.

—*Do you? All I smell is shit and vomit.*

Charles was experimenting with vulgar language of the kind he'd been exposed to for months in close confinement with his fellow man. He found it distasteful and decided to abandon it as alien to his nature.

—*That's the trouble with you, brother,* David said. *You lack the soul of a poet.*

Two years of back-bending labor and sharing their tent with rats and ticks netted enough glittery dust for a holiday back East, where a man could buy an egg without pawning his watch; but New York without its entertainments was little improvement over the camp, and the dust ran out like sand in an hourglass. During the return trip to San Francisco, David developed a cough and a sore throat which by journey's end had turned into racking agony, spitting blood, chills, fever, and sudden release. Charles buried him in Yerba Buena Cemetery and returned to the fields, for the solitary reason that it was the plan they'd agreed on; neither one had thought beyond spending their wealth once they had it.

By then, the big concerns had bought up all the good

prospects and squeezed out the miners hoping to nibble a living round the edges. The miners had tried banding together, but though they outnumbered the enemy, they hadn't the reserves to weather a boycott from the freighting firms that had thrown in with the conglomerates; Wells, Fargo and its competitors simply refused to ship their ore, and starved them out as systematically as Washington did the Indians. Charles was gone by the time they gave up and went back to work for others; his heart was never in a fight that couldn't be won. He walked away, leaving behind his tent, skillet, pickaxes, and a sack half full of beans hard and dry as pebbles, and was still walking three weeks later. The habit by that time had taken hold; he was bound for New York by way of a stout pair of legs and soles calloused thick as slabs of salt pork.

He didn't get that far. In Decatur, Illinois, he met and married sixteen-year-old Elizabeth Johnson, who bore him three daughters, Ida, Eva, and Frances. He supported his family by farming a patch of sorry ground he bought with the last of what he'd saved on train fare. There being no market in rocks, they went hungry most of the time. While in town to look for odd jobs, he stopped before a platform built of green pine decked with red-white-and-blue bunting, shared by a leather-lunged local politician in a striped and swollen waistcoat and a handsome young woman in a nurse's cap and cape, offering wages of thirteen dollars a month and a basket of fried chicken to each man who stepped forward and signed on to defend the Union from southern rabble. He joined, as much for the chicken as for the wages; he'd foregone three days of meals in order to keep his girls from starvation.

That was how Charles Bolton came to serve with Company B of the 116th Illinois Volunteer Infantry; and to regret, while fighting in Mississippi and Arkansas—and particularly while lying flat on his back in Dallas, Georgia, draining pus from a stomach torn open by a Minié ball into a white-enamel basin—a decision made on the basis of an empty belly and a light head.

He survived the shock, trauma, and (that greatest killer of the war) peritonitis, and fought—in sergeant's stripes now—at Vicksburg, Chattanooga, Kenesaw Mountain, and against the backdrop of Sherman's Inferno in Atlanta, where he received a battlefield promotion to second lieutenant; but Lee's surrender came faster than his bars.

Bolton little regretted it. The whole transaction was blood and sweat and drenching rain, mosquitoes the size of horseflies, horseflies the size of hummingbirds, and rats twice as big as they grew them in California. He came out of the hostilities with only a scar to show for his near-fatal injury, but chronic bad feet, the arches broken from marching and toes which, once frostbitten, froze again in a fraction of the time in temperatures half as cold; bad feet, and the determination never again to let himself get so hungry as to impair his good judgment.

He walked, corns and all, from Washington, D.C., back to Illinois, reunited with his family, and with his savings from army duty and the pittance he realized from selling his all-but-worthless farm, moved bag and baggage, wife and daughters, to New Oregon, Iowa, and a better tract of land. But the work was as hard and the profits scarcely enough to put bread on the table and clothes on their backs.

The mining bug was like yellow fever; it kept recurring

just when one thought he'd put it behind. Before dawn one day in 1867, tempted by stories of silver in Montana, he packed supplies and provisions and set off on foot for Idaho, and after sinking a dry shaft there, to a camp called Silver Bow. The name was promising; the prospects were not.

> Dear Lizzie [he wrote],
>     Your wayfarer is on his way home . . .

Whether he changed his mind or got confused as to his directions is not known, for he hiked west. He wrote home from time to time, which impressed unschooled prospectors, who paid him to draft letters for them. (His talents as a scribe were developing.) He sent some of this money home, but it was insufficient. His remorse drove him to seek more frequent employment, shoveling out stables and loading sacks of grain. His stop in the Mormon capital of Salt Lake City was brief: Little work was to be found by gentiles.

Sometime during this period, he fell out of the habit of sending money home. James B. Hume would make much of this later, to quell further romanticism of the "lyrical larcenist" by the ravenous press; his own victory tasted like ashes. The explanation may be less simple than common abandonment. Perhaps the decision came from shame and despair, or a comforting letter he'd received from Elizabeth (comforting, but possibly false encouragement, or a weary dismissal born of eternal waiting), saying that she'd begun to take in sewing and was earning a reputation for fine work among the discerning better class of woman in Cedar Rapids and Des Moines.

Or . . .

Or because his life back East had faded to resemble something he'd dreamed only, or a story related to him by a fellow Yankee waiting out a bombardment in a crater dug by a Confederate mortar. War, hardship, and loss assumed a reality apart from all others. Almost certainly, the farther Charles Bolton drifted toward the setting sun, the more vivid grew the memory of his ventures with brother David.

Whatever his motives, he sacked up his possibles once again and resumed walking until he ran clear out of continent, finding himself back in California's Mother Lode country.

He stopped in Yerba Buena to pay his respects to Davy; but did not go from there to the fields. A reading man from youth, schooled by his English parents in Shakespeare's sonnets, Donne's poetry and sermons, and serializations of Dickens, his grammar, syntax, and vocabulary sharpened by his experiences in writing letters, he applied for and obtained the job of teaching grade school, first in Sierra County, then in neighboring Contra Costa. He found pleasure in the lessons he gave, but either his enthusiasm for the material was not shared by the children and grandchildren of his fellow Forty-Niners—a largely illiterate lot, as he well remembered—or he lacked the educator's gift for translating his affection to his students. In 1875, after Decoration Day, he collected his salary and invested in a shotgun.

On July 26 of that year, a solitary gunman dressed in a linen duster and a hood made from a flour sack stepped out from behind a boulder on the Reynolds Ferry road in Calaveras County on a spot called Funk Hill, and invited the driver of a mud wagon to "Please throw down the box."

If Wells, Fargo never forgot, neither did Black Bart.

# ELEVEN

*Jim Hume was a manhunter with no one to match;*
*nor has any arrived who can equal his catch.*
*Yet like Bart he eschewed the horse as his mode;*
*for a plain oak desk was the steed that he rode.*

Two decades of farm life had palled on the man born
as Charles E. Boles; so it was with his nemesis. At age
twenty-three, James B. Hume left his plow standing
in its furrow on his father's farm in La Grange, Indiana, to
answer the golden cry from California.

As it was with so many others—Black Bart included—
his destiny was thus determined, but in the end was directed
more by the labor of his wits than of his back.

In the autumn of 1850, just as the Boles brothers set their
feet for the first time on the North Fork of the American
River, Hume rode into a log settlement colorfully christened
Hangtown, in honor of the bountiful local harvest of claim-
jumpers, highwaymen, horse thieves, man-killers, and ped-
erasts strung from trees like hops hung up to cure. Later it
became Old Dry Diggings—a designation hurled back bit-
terly over the shoulders of busted miners on the return

journey to civilization and work-for-hire—and finally Placerville; but by the time sufficient gold had been excavated to earn the more promising name, Hume was no longer looking for it. Like Fergus Callahan, Dail's father and founder of the family dry-goods business, he'd opened a store, first to supplement his prospecting, then as a substitute to it, selling his worn-out gear and bucket of sourdough to some starry-eyed greenhorn and investing the proceeds in genuine glass windows and a broader selection of merchandise.

It was in this phase of his life that Hume developed the practice of keeping elaborate records. Not being one to turn his face from unpleasant fact, he faithfully logged each debit as it was incurred, deducted the amount from the figures in black, noted the difference (frequently preceded by a minus) at the bottom of each page, and set down the grim total at the end of the month. By this means he determined down to the date how much longer he could remain in business.

That date was the last Saturday in December 1854, when he sold the last of his fixtures at auction and signed over the deed to the lot his log store stood on to a newcomer from Baltimore, who'd made the trip west not to mine, but to speculate in real property, and needed the building for his office. The transisthmian railroad was nearing completion across Panama, eliminating the necessity to sail ten thousand miles around the horn in order to reach California. He intended to be among the first to greet pilgrims using the swift new route to transplant themselves in San Francisco.

Hume reckoned the man would make a killing, but he felt no envy. He'd had his life's portion of telling people to have a pleasant day when he himself was not, or when the

THE BALLAD OF BLACK BART ★ 99

person he was telling it to was someone he'd just as soon see off to hell on the Sunset Limited. In any event, he had a job, one that didn't involve wrapping parcels in paper, binding them with string, and climbing ladders to hoist pails of lard off the top shelf. (Carpenters insisted on making more space between the top shelves than the bottom, forcing merchants to store the larger and heavier items near the ceiling; he suspected they were in league with the quacks in Chinatown you paid to jump up and down on your throbbing back; he'd not miss the place.) The prospect of nursemaiding carriageloads of tenderfeet through miles of scrubland, scouting for building sites, held no more appeal, whatever the profit.

With the population spreading like wildflowers after a rain, the El Dorado County sheriff was hard pressed to pay calls on all the landowners who owed taxes. With the anticipated new deluge of settlers by way of Panama, he was looking at more time spent in the saddle than at home with his wife and children. He was a fat man, but the extra upholstery didn't bring much comfort to tenting on the old campground; and a diet of beans and bacon did little to relieve his gout. When, while ordering a sack of oats for his spavined mount, he complained of the situation to Hume, the storekeeper asked him why he didn't delegate the chore to his deputies.

"They'd like that, sure as shit," said the lawman. "See, I get to keep a percentage of what I collect, and I'd have to divide it up among them. I'm a family man, and new shoes don't grow on trees."

That was how James B. Hume came to be sworn in as deputy sheriff in charge of collecting taxes. He kept his records in such intricate detail the amounts were never questioned, and he worked solely on salary. Naturally this delighted the sheriff, who came to rely on him more than all his other deputies combined. So in 1864, when a gang of Copperheads robbed a stage at Bullion Bend in his jurisdiction, Hume led the posse that ran them to ground, took them into custody, recovered money earmarked for the Confederate war fund, and returned it to Wells, Fargo, & Co. He was promoted to under-sheriff, next in line to the most important office in the county. Four years later, he ran against his superior and was elected sheriff.

Wells, Fargo never forgets. After another four years spent tracking and shackling road agents who had preyed on Company strongboxes, Sheriff Hume received an invitation from John J. Valentine, general superintendent of operations, to meet him in the San Francisco office.

It was his first visit to the brick building with its deceptively narrow front in the city's famed Fireproof Block. He was impressed with how much space it commanded, extending all the way to the street paralleling Montgomery; and particularly the banks of oaken file cases in all the upstairs rooms. His faith in thorough and accurate records had proven to be of more value than days and nights in the saddle or the Yellow Boy Winchester he carried in a boot when he was on the scent. (Had his overstuffed predecessor been aware of that, it was likely Hume would still be stocking tins on shelves belonging to someone else.)

The superintendent, for his part, was even more impressed with his guest. Himself a physical specimen to attract note, stout of build and elaborately bearded, with a Mason's ring on his left little finger, Valentine greeted a tall, distinguished-looking man of erect bearing: He was groomed carefully and polite, but not to the point of seeming obsequious. Although the black felt hat he removed upon entering the room was nondescript—one might even say it was drab, at a time when men of distinction paid particular attention to their accessories—his host surmised that he wore it more to draw attention away from his physical presence than to invite it; a modest man, then, the antithesis of the strutting pistoleros in Beadle's Dime Library of sensational fiction. Their previous encounters had been of short duration, and the superintendent preoccupied at the time with the details of specific robberies. On this occasion he'd been concerned with the Company's public profile should it include a peacock like Wild Bill or that truculent crowd in Dodge City and Tombstone.

With his trim handlebars streaked with gray, silver watch chain, tidy dress, freshly blacked boots, and organ-pipe arrangement of cigars in a plated case in his breast pocket, Hume might have been taken for a banker or an attorney but for the badge of office pinned to his waistcoat. If he wore a revolver, it wasn't evident. His responses to questions were equally reassuring, quiet, brief, and to the point; on matters regarding the business of convicting captives of the crimes they were charged with, he was surprisingly learned, nearly as much as the legal experts whom Wells, Fargo kept on retainer. He understood more than most of the Company's field agents that it was one thing to catch a man red-handed, another to overcome the hurdles erected by attorneys for the defense. Compliments on his successes as a peace officer he turned away with a somewhat impatient gesture and a swift change of subject.

He was loquacious on one point only: his method of operation in regard to the plundering plague that had turned the coach roads into a Robbers Roost.

"Mind you," opened Valentine, "I cannot have these villains slaughtered in frequent gun battles, or hanging like crepe from every tree in perdition, much as the picture appeals to me. The eastern press does not scruple between violence committed by bandits and violence committed against them. That kind of thing frightens away settlers, which disinclines investment by the great mining interests, which are butter to the Company's bread."

Hereupon the sheriff's moustaches stretched at the corners; the closest thing to a smile he'd yet shown. "I believe I can assuage your hesitation on that account, sir. Give me but a flat surface and an unlimited supply of paper and ink, and I shall deliver results without unnecessary carnage. No two miscreants are the same; each leaves his mark, as personal as a footprint or a signature. Most of the arrests I helped bring about took place in saloons and bath houses, where they were traced after I and my people had gathered sufficient evidence to identify them. A thief riddled with holes and put on display at the undertaker's is a sign of failure on the part of justice. My intention is to make that a rare event. In eight years I've not fired a gun except in practice." He inclined his graying head toward the row of file cases running the length of the long wall facing the side-street. "Those are my weapons of choice. When it comes to bringing a criminal career to a close, they're as sure as a coffin."

That ended the interview. The superintendent had made his decision, without consulting either the Messrs. Wells or Fargo. He offered James B. Hume the position of chief of

detectives in charge of investigating robberies and embez-
zlements perpetrated against the Company.

"In the matter of wages, I think you will find we're at
least as generous as the taxpayers of El Dorado."

"That's of small interest. I am a bachelor. I lack for places
to spend what I earn at present."

"Welcome aboard, Chief." Valentine rose from behind
his desk and offered his hand.

Hume stood and accepted it. "I thank you, sir. I'll notify
the county of my decision to resign."

# TWELVE

*If only God can make gold shine,*
*and the Devil make Man to say, "It's mine";*
*it took a Bart to make Hume cry,*
*pierce a vein, and bleed Wells, Fargo dry.*

The lumberman smelled of fresh-sawn wood and clean sweat, with a fusty finish; he'd come to Hume's office directly after stabling his buckboard and pair in San Francisco. The ponderous lumber wagon and massive Percherons remained home in Butte County. The frock coat he wore over a flannel shirt was turned at the cuffs, and months spent interred in cedar and moth-flakes clung to it like an uncollected debt. Apart from that, the man looked prosperous enough. His face and hands were scrubbed, leaving only cross-hatchings of old dirt earned through honest labor, and his stout boots put the chief of detectives in mind of the man he'd invited the visitor in to discuss. (Baron and bandit alike knew the importance of looking after one's feet.) The trade in California hardwood was fast approaching the market in bullion.

"You say this fellow was sitting on a rock writing. What was he writing?"

"I cannot say. I did not get that close. From his look, it might have been his last will and testament."

"Old?"

"That; and tuckered out."

"And you saw no horse or other transportation?"

"Not a sign."

"Unless someone dropped him off, it might explain his condition. What else did you see?"

"An old blanket roll, which was lumpy enough to contain his belongings. Mind, I thought little of it at first, except that he was up to mischief. That stretch of country is notorious for—"

"I heard something of the sort. The robbery of the Ukiah stage took place almost a week ago. Why did you wait that long to come here, if you're so interested in the bounty?"

"He appeared all-in, as I said, so I dismissed him as a hazard. I did not learn of the robbery until a few days later. Considering that it took place on that very—"

" 'Gray of whiskers and hair, wrinkled face, drooping shoulders.' " Hume read from the visitor's dictation to Thacker, his secretary. "This is far from the description of the man who held up the coach and demanded the surrender of the express box. I could take a dozen men off the top of any freight car that rolls into the city who would answer it, and turn them over to the police on a vagrancy charge."

"I thought along the same lines, which is another reason why I did not report straightaway. There is still the matter of *where* I saw him."

Hume barked an order to Thacker, sitting at the desk facing his. In moments a leather portfolio pregnant with its contents was deposited atop the heap in front of his superior. Hume patted it without reaching for the tie. "All these people are ahead of you in line," he told the lumberman. "Tramps, odd-looking strangers, neighbors, and relatives who have offended them in some way—all of them Black Bart, to hear them tell it. If there's a kernel of truth in one report out of a dozen, Wells and Fargo would have to divvy up the eight hundred dollars it's offering at a mean amount of seven dollars and sixty cents per person." He laid his cigar in its tray to smolder and stood, thrusting out his hand. "Thank you for your effort. Leave your address with my secretary, and if anything comes of it, the Company will be in touch. Wells, Fargo never forgets."

"It never pays up, either." The lumberman left without shaking hands or stopping at the other desk.

"Was that necessary?" asked Thacker, when they were alone. "So far he's the only one to offer an account of anyone perched so close to the site and time of a robbery, and he saw him *writing*."

"Unfortunately, the level of literacy here has improved since the days of forty-nine. We haven't the time or space to corral every man who can string words into a sentence, even if it turns out he has a flair for verse."

"Still, we could give the information to the press."

"To what value? It would only stir up the hornets. The description favors half the male population of the state."

The other glanced down at the sheet he'd written on. "It favors you, if you take no offense to that."

Hume's moustaches, noticeably whiter in recent weeks,

stood out against the deep scarlet of his face. "Then arrest me, you damn pup, and see if you can collect."

"Very sorry, sir." He returned to his station. It was unlike Hume to lose his temper over an idle remark. However much or little Bart had stolen from the Company, he'd taken a significant bite out of the chief's thick hide.

\* \* \*

John J. Valentine pulled a face at the foreign object squatting in the center of his Brussels carpet. He prided himself on keeping a tidy office, never going home at the end of the day until his desk was clear of everything but a crisp new green blotter sheet and the glob of bronze inkwell Wells and Fargo had presented him with on the occasion of his fifth anniversary with the Company, and which he used for a paperweight; he dictated all his communications to his secretary, who transposed them from Pitman shorthand to a Remington type-writing machine, and always brought in a gravity pen for his employer to sign them. Before turning out the lamps, the general superintendent squared all corners, glanced about, and pronounced himself satisfied.

The intruder, a homely box bound with strap iron, was clean enough, but its unabashedly utilitarian appearance— twenty inches long, twelve inches wide, and ten inches deep, secured with a hasp and padlock, and painted Wells, Fargo's trademark deep green shade—belonged in the counting-room downstairs, awaiting filling with coins or notes and transfer to the front boot of a mud-wagon, and not in the room where Valentine spent all of his working day. Nothing like it had ever presented itself above the ground floor. The yoke-shouldered teamsters his chief of detectives had enlisted to carry it up the stairs stood back from it now, breathing heavily and sweating in sheets.

This was the same room where six years before a somewhat less well-fed executive had interviewed a somewhat less grizzled applicant for the security job; and while this was not the first time Valentine had felt a twinge of doubt about his choice—there was the affair of the "Never Forgets" headstone that had made his own distant employers bilious, and the business of inviting the creatures of the press into the ranks of the Company's undercover agents—it suggested to him that perhaps Hume's preoccupation with the atrocities committed by Black Bart had unhinged his usually sanguine powers of reason: Recent witnesses claimed Bart had begun telling drivers farewell and to "Give my kind regards to Jim Hume," in place of a poem. It was enough to bring a flush to the face of the man in the moon.

"What does it signify?" Valentine asked. "Do you imagine this is the first time I've set eyes on one of our express boxes?"

"You've never set eyes on one like this. What do you reckon it's made of?"

"Oak, of course. I authorized the expenditure myself, against the advice of the owls who keep the accounts, who pressed for pine."

"And what persuaded you?"

"Jim, you stretch my patience. Hardwood's stouter, more difficult for bandits to break into, and so heavy as to be cumbersome to carry away on horseback."

"It was a sound decision; and an inspiration to me, when I commissioned this one."

"Is it your responsibility? I should think you've enough

to attend to without interfering in the gear-and-pulley end of the operation."

Hume, standing beside the box, leaned down and rapped the lid with his knuckles. It made a deep gong. The oak had never sprouted that could manage that knell. Valentine blew out his whiskers.

"A strongbox built of iron? Shall we crack the back of every driver with the line?"

"Not if he takes his time about loading it. The men who would relieve him of it haven't that luxury. John, we've had this conversation: A minute lost to the thief is a minute won for us. It can take as much as forty for him to break free the booty from this box, and that's a mile to the good."

Valentine chuckled. "Why not furnish the coach with a proper safe, and pounce on the beggars while they're still at it?"

"That was to be my next suggestion, on routes involving substantial cargo in coins and bullion, bolted to the floor."

"You would have us spend a thousand dollars to prevent the loss of a hundred."

"We do that every time we offer a bounty five times in excess of what was stolen." Hume kicked the box, eliciting another hollow boom and moving it not at all. "The cost will diminish in direct ratio to the loss. Inside of six months, a robbery in sourdough territory will be as rare as an honest man in Sacramento."

The superintendent, who on occasion played cards with Governor Stanford, winced at the suggestion inherent in that remark. "I would dislike to dismiss with the services of Mr. Ayer. He has served us since the beginning, and his cabinetry skills are superb."

Joseph William Ayer, San Francisco's most celebrated cabinetmaker, had been commissioned to design and construct the boxes from early days.

"I've heard him complain often about repeating the same project over and again," Hume said. "It's not like building a custom desk or lady's dressing-table. In any event, the traffic from Panama will require him to hire additional apprentices just to keep up with the demand for rocking chairs and mahogany banisters. He'll never miss us. Meanwhile any old man who can manage an axe or a hatchet can open a wooden crate in a single swing."

Hume's thoughts were still on the description the lumberman had given him of the weary traveler on the Ukiah road. He'd found it more credible than he'd let on to his secretary, but of only nebulous use in the conduct of the investigation. The picture of a predator from whom youth was fleeting, however, had led him to the concept of a container for transporting valuable shipments that would challenge the strength of a middle-aged man. He'd engaged the services of the forger who supplied the iron straps for Ayer's boxes, paying for the materials and labor out of his own pocket. The unimaginative Valentine was nearly impossible to convince with words alone.

Now, as he watched the superintendent hoist himself from his high-backed swivel, circle his desk—which unlike his own was bare enough to set out a twenty-piece tea service—and bend down against the pressure of his spreading paunch to sound his own knuckle-note on the box, he knew the argument was won.

But the victory was only slightly less hollow than the reverberating sound from inside the empty vessel. In the time the item was under construction, Black Bart had thrown down his damned shotgun on three stagecoaches three weeks apart—and he'd broadened his operations across the line to include Oregon. He was now wanted in two states, as much as ever was Jesse James, and more than Billy the Kid.

# THIRTEEN

*When a man robs another, he bargains his life;*
*agrees to pay interest in personal strife.*
*The bill when it's due takes a terrible toll:*
*the robber must close out the debt with his soul.*

O n June 14, 1882, Thomas Forse dug his bootheels into
the footboards, hauled back on the lines, and set the
brake, his heart tum-tum-tumming like a kettle
drum in his breast. The horses snorted and tossed their
heads, annoyed at the sudden interruption. The stupid
beasts, which shied at so much as a blown page from a discarded newspaper, made no connection with the figure
who'd stepped into their path and mortal danger. That his
head was covered by a flour-sack hood and he was pointing
the twin muzzles of a sawn-off shotgun at the man on the
seat meant no more to them than a shift in the wind.

The spot was three miles from Little Lake; the stage had
come just that far on its way toward Ukiah, a name that in
the journals had come to be followed almost exclusively by
the modifier "robbery." Forse's own brother, Harry, a fellow
driver, had been stopped within hailing distance of that

location only six months before, by a man similarly masked and armed. It occurred to him in the moment that his family had been singled out by dark faith and Black Bart.

"Please throw down the box"; had he actually heard the words, or had he supplied them himself from his imagination based on Harry's report? Not wishing to risk his skin on a misunderstanding, he spoke:

"I can't."

The front of the flour sack caved in and bellied. The man who wore it had drawn in and expelled his breath in sharp exasperation. "Throw down the damn box or I'll blow your goddamned head off!"

This could not be Bart, whose cordial good manners were as notorious as his nickname. A wave of fresh panic overtook Forse like the ague.

"It's bolted d-down, I meant t-to say." He stammered on the dentals. As if to prove his claim, he lifted his feet from the boards, where no box could be seen. "In the back."

The head inside the sack rotated a quarter-turn that direction. There came a moment when the man who belonged to it appeared to be studying the scales: on one side, salvation, on the other, a tug on the triggers and a burial plot arranged through the generosity of Wells, Fargo, & Co., with all the obsequious trimmings.

The bastards.

"Step down."

Forse's legs were nearly useless: They'd gone to sleep or, more accurately, fallen into a swoon. Steadying himself with a hand on the wing of the seat, he lowered his weight to the ground carefully, lest he stumble and startle the man into discharging a round into his face. At last he stood, still using the support of the mud wagon. His thighs and calves stung as if he'd waded through a field of nettles.

The shotgun—an extension of the bandit's arms—lifted. It took the man in front of it a full second to grasp the grim certainty: The bandit had decided to make good on the threat of decapitation. He squeezed his lids shut, expecting the blast: Would he hear it? None had returned from the Beyond to furnish the intelligence.

He didn't hear it; but only because it didn't come. The gesture meant only that his hands must be raised.

Forse complied, chilled and enfevered from equal parts relief and dread, and stood quivering as the gunman freed a hand from his weapon and slid it under the sheep lining of the driver's jacket, sliding his palm down the right side of his torso, around his waist, and up the other side. The side-by-side bores of the shotgun remained steady, so close to Forse's face the sharp scent of oil sizzled the hairs in his nostrils. From time to time the eyes showing through the holes cut in the sack—pale blue they were, cold as nickel steel—shifted toward the passengers, who remained still, their harsh breathing audible for yards. The voice of insanity whispered to him to sweep his own hands down, grasp the barrels, and wrest the gun free. He'd be alive, to begin with, and a hero to boot, sure as—

Custer.

The voice of sanity bellowed to him to remain still, adding, "You shit-brained fool!" loud enough to be heard outside his skull.

A century he stood thus; one second more and he might have thrown in on the side of lunacy, the way a man with no particular reason to end his life might yield to the tingling temptation to let himself fall forward off the edge of a precipice.

Or so, for the rest of his days, he summed up the course of his reasoning to anyone who gave him an ear. In fact, the decision had come down to the simple fact that as an employee of the Company, the coins and notes in the iron box meant no more to him than Confederate graybacks. Let Wells and Fargo stick out their own necks for something to which he had no title.

The passengers, three men and two women, were murmuring among themselves; at a motion of the weapon, they fell silent, with a tiny squeak from one of the women; or just as likely from one of the men. Another gesture and they alighted, hands raised without being ordered.

"Unhitch the team."

Forse hesitated, then gathered the lines, unbuckled the straps and traces, and led the horses forward by the left lead's bit-chain. The brute tried to jerk loose. Fear and rage brought it a forearm blow across the cheekstrap from its master. It wall-eyed him, but complied. When Forse stopped, Flour Sack made a sweeping motion with the shotgun, which the passengers interpreted correctly as a command to join the driver.

"If any of you is armed, surrender your weapon now. I won't ask again."

Clothing rustled. A long-barreled Colt and a pocket pistol raised puffs of dust from the earth, followed by a derringer from a lady's handbag. Forse prayed there were no holdouts.

"Now walk down the road, all of you, and around the

bend. Bring the team. If you come back in less than an hour, you'll have no more need of horse or coach."

The highwayman stood with his back to the empty vehicle, the shotgun level and braced against a hip. Not a word rose from the group as they accompanied the horses toward a bootjack some thirty yards in the direction of Ukiah.

Bolton waited a minute—by his fifty-dollar gold watch—after he could no longer see them, then lowered his gun, and stepped around the boulder he'd hidden behind. He swept off his hood and stuffed it in his pocket. From his tattered blanket roll he extracted an iron maul and a steel bar with a chiseled bit. He'd read in the *Herald* of the Company's improved security measures and had come prepared.

Rather than bother unbolting the iron box from the rear boot, he mounted the metal step provided for the laborers who loaded the baggage and went to work, the blows of the hammer against the butt of the wrecking bar ringing off the firs and hardwoods walling the road. It was backbreaking work, burning his muscles and slicking him with sweat from his hairline to the soles of his feet in their stout boots. It took the better part of the hour before the box yielded anything more than its shape; he had to work swiftly then, and hang his fatigue.

He'd had to shift the extra load from one arm to the other throughout his long hike; the effort, and the anticipation of the burden that awaited him, had been as much responsible for his uncharacteristic discourtesy, and this, too—his abandonment of the lessons associated with good breeding—had compounded his impatience.

The harvest was decent, two hundred and change in

double eagles, cartwheel dollars, and promissory notes, plus another substantial draft in the mail pouch (which he left; he'd been too cautious the last time to enter a bank in the person of Charles E. Bolton or his alias, T. Z. Spaulding, and attempt to convert it to cash); but the physical effort involved was little better than assaulting rock-hard ground with pick and shovel for paltry returns, and he was no longer as young as the piss-and-vinegar farm lad who'd tried his luck thirty years ago. He hastened away from the battered box before the others could return, and hadn't the sand in him even to hum his favorite air.

He rested in the mountains, soaking his feet and his aching body in streams, brewing coffee in the same tins he'd emptied of beans, and eating them cold and foregoing hot drink when he sensed someone was near and might investigate the smell of a fire and cooking. He did not miss San Francisco's entertainments during this sabbatical; the bare business of maintaining a camp left him drained. He'd be poor company at dinner or in the balcony at the opera. At night he lay on his back, eyes open and picking out the constellations he knew the names of until his lids grew heavy and he slept. In the mornings his muscles retained the memory of each protrusion in the earth. Summers can be cold in high country: His breath smoked most mornings and his fingers stiffened, the knuckles swollen and red. Nearly a month passed before he arose feeling a tiny bit better than he had the day before.

On July 13, refreshed at last, he rolled his necessaries inside his blanket and descended once again to the coach roads.

He stopped the LaPorte-to-Ortonville stage near Strawberry, and saw at once that the pickings were good. There was a shotgun messenger—one George W. Hackett, the *Herald* later reported—and Wells, Fargo's frugality permitted the expense only when the risk of loss was high. The giddy anticipation of a major triumph got the better of Bolton's native caution. When the driver lost his grip on the express box, dropping it with a report to the boards, the noise took his eyes away from the armed man. The shell in the barrel Hackett fired first was a slug; it tore Bolton's hood and ploughed a furrow across his right temple. It burned like a blacksmith's iron and dumped blood into his eye; he thought himself blind. He swung about and ran.

Ran for what seemed miles, swiping away blood with the sleeve of his duster, before panic gave way to exhaustion and he sank to the ground. His heart was trip-hammering.

*Why?* Did the dunderpate not know it wasn't *his* money? The world had turned over onto its head.

When he'd managed to staunch the bleeding with his handkerchief, he got up, retraced his steps, and found his blanket and gear undisturbed where he'd left it. The coach was gone, and with it his flour sack, to join a handful of dried peach pits in Jim Hume's collection.

For the first time in twenty-three outings, Bolton had been forced to flee for his life, and with only a gash in his scalp to show for the ordeal.

Useless to doubt it: The outlaw life had commenced to lose its poetry.

# FOURTEEN

*Years of success in his chosen black art*
*had pumped up the legend of Mr. Black Bart;*
*years of vain labor by Hume and the law*
*had rubbed and worn their character raw.*

J im, will you for the love of God leave the blasted thing alone? You'll wear it out and it will be no use as evidence."

Sheriff Ben Thorn sprawled in the Morris chair in the parlor of his palace in San Andreas, scowling at James Hume and turning a tumbler of Kentucky rye around and around inside his fist. His square-booted feet were planted on a Turkish rug in a large room that seemed small because of all the furniture his wife had managed to stuff into it, leaving only narrow avenues of passage between pedestal tables, music box, china cabinet, grand piano, settees, and a thousand-year-old bust of a prosperous Roman merchant on a pedestal. The place he'd been so proud to bring his bride home to in 1859 had begun to suffocate him.

James Hume ignored his protest, toying with the flour sack recovered from the robbery attempt near Strawberry, poking his fingers through the eyeholes and stroking the crust of dried blood with the ball of a thumb. He'd taken to carrying it about with him everywhere he went, like a magic talisman that must lead him eventually to the man who'd worn it. "Do you suppose he perished up there?"

"If he did, some sourdough will stumble on his bones, depend on it." Thorn drank. He was imbibing more now and eating less. His appetite had deserted him, taking with it the comforts of inebriation. The stuff had no more effect on his mood than mineral water. He'd survived decades of innuendo in respect to his lavish place of dwelling, only to win re-election most recently by a narrow plurality. Seven years of steady plunder by the damn scribbling rascal, and the sheriffs of a dozen counties and Wells, Fargo's vaunted sleuth were no closer to laying hands on him than they had been at the start. Thorn was painted a fat incompetent in a golden cage, and it was no comfort that his companion showed few signs of worry on his own behalf. Surely the Company was as impatient as the press and the public for a finish to the thing.

"I'd hate for that to be the case," said the detective. "It would be like coming to the end of a book only to find the last page is missing."

"I care not, so long as we come to the end. What are the great men saying?"

"Just now Mr. Wells and Mr. Fargo are kicking up a fuss round Hackett, the shotgun messenger. I shouldn't be surprised if the journals call for him to replace me." He chuckled.

"How in thunder can you joke of it? You are too old to be out scouting for employment."

"I may hang it up anyway; but only once I've twisted my hand inside Bart's collar." He wrung the sack. "Life will be drab once I've managed that."

"I shouldn't mind a little drabness."

They sat in silence, Thorn refilling his glass from time to time from the square cut-crystal decanter and siphon on the table at his elbow, Hume fingering the stained sack and lighting his succession of cigars. The room took on a fug of alcohol fumes and tobacco-smoke. Anna Thorn would complain, upon returning from her charity work, that the place smelled like a low tavern.

The sheriff reopened his favorite subject. "You ought to be concerned, for your sake as well as for mine. This makes three-and-twenty times Bart's nicked the Company."

"Twenty-two. I'm not persuaded it was he at Little Lake. That fellow was a brute."

"Because he neglected to say, 'Please' and 'Thank you'? Perhaps his courtesy has ebbed away along with his poetic spirit. What would you select to rhyme with 'I'll blow your goddamn head off'?"

"Anyone can obtain a flour sack and carve holes in it. The man who left this one behind, turning tail at the first shot fired in anger without returning fire, is our man. I wonder if that gun of his is even loaded. Hum." He pumped locomotive gusts into the murk, considering the matter.

"If it wasn't before, you can be sure it is now. If our man is losing his gentleman's manners, it may not be such a bad thing. If he wings or slays an employee or a passenger, perhaps the press will stop writing of him as if he were some kind of Lochinvar."

"It would seem to be a very bad thing for the victim,"

said the other, scowling into the pall; but the suggestion in-trigued him for a moment. He shook his head. "Once these fellows have their teeth into an idea, it's the same to them as gospel. They'll sing his praises till trumpet's blow. He could be photographed strangling Jenny Lind on the stage of the Grand Opera House and they would claim he gallantly came forward to save her from choking on a herring-bone. No, Ben, I think our only course is to run him to ground."

"Capital. I was certain you'd arrive at a solution to all the evils that beset us. Now all we need is a way to bring the thing about."

"How does one go about flushing a badger from its bur-row?"

"That's easy. Smoke him out."

"That would be feckless. Badgers always dig an escape tunnel. You post a man at both ends and wait him out."

"But where is Bart's burrow?"

"Somewhere close, I'm bound. I feel it in our bones. Where would a man who has made such easy gains go to spend them, if not San Francisco?"

"That's a mighty large burrow."

"Patience will shrink it in time."

Thorn took a large swig and wobbled it around his mouth before committing it to his throat; the burn when it reached his stomach was more satisfying when he let the liquid come to body temperature. "Of course, the stumbling-block with Patience is it's a game that must be played alone."

* * *

He wore a patch of sticking-plaster on his temple for six weeks, and took care to keep his head covered in public view. The wound needed stitches to avoid permanence, but he dare not consult a physician; his scrape with shotgun messenger Hackett had been reported, and spread through every telegraph column in the country, and whatever Hippocrates had had to say about the seal of the profession, it was gossamer compared to the greenbacks Wells, Fargo was offering for Black Bart's capture and conviction. He was not a religious man, but he prayed that the hair would grow back and conceal the wound.

His companions during this period noted that Charlie Bolton was uncharacteristically moody. Neither Matt Leacock nor Alec Fitzhugh could draw him out with the usual banter about racing and prizefighting, and their companion's gift for the humorous anecdote seemed to have abandoned him. He was drinking more as well; sometimes as many as three brandies over supper, and the neck of a miniature calabash flask poked from a waistcoat pocket. He spoke little, and only in response to something directed at him, ate even less, and left them to their desserts with a few perfunctory words of farewell.

"Mr. Bolton?"

He'd started past the cloakroom without thought of his coat. The girl paled a little when he jumped at the sound of his name, but said nothing, even when he scraped a nickel across the counter and shrugged into the garment on his way out without a word or the lines of poetry she'd come to look forward to as a respite from the tedium of her job. She pouted at his back, and had to be addressed twice by the next customer before turning to redeem his coat check.

"D'you think the Panic affected his mines?" Fitzhugh asked.

Leacock doctored his milk with port. "I shouldn't think. Things have eased up considerable, with Chet Arthur in office; he's a friend to business and don't gouge too much for a favor. The trade in cattle couldn't be better."

"Whale oil's improving. For a while there I was afraid they were burning tallow on Fifth Avenue."

"The rich are always the first to complain when the screws tighten."

"Not working stiffs like you and me, eh?" Fitzhugh grinned, flicking a crumb of cake from a lapel. "We aren't exactly lining up outside the Salvation Army, and neither is Charlie. Like all those mining pioneers he's stuffed his mattress with bundles."

"No doubt; though he's taken on bad manners. I never knew him to leave his hat on indoors."

\* \* \*

Truth be told, he was not so much disheartened as worn out. The close transaction near Strawberry had cost him sleep, but the lesson had been worth the tutor's price, lest he blunder into his own grave: If there are two men sharing the driver's seat, stay behind your boulder and wait for the next coach, like any city commuter who'd missed one trolley and must hold his soul in check waiting for the next. The sheer chore of cracking Wells, Fargo's new boxes was a trial, and sleeping on the ground under the stars (and in drenching rain and sometimes bitter snow) was a young man's sport, before the skin began to thin and rheumatism filled his joints with chalk.

Although he couldn't know what they'd discussed when he was absent, Leacock and Fitzhugh had hit close to the mark regarding his change of humor, but they'd had it backward: It was the improvement of the country's economic situation since the Panic that had dampened his spirits, not the reverse. Settlers who a few years before had thought nothing of putting up a stranger for the night, blaming his itinerant habits on the scarcity of paying employment, now peered at him with rancor and, worse, suspicion when he showed up at their door with his tattered blanket roll asking for a roof. They saw him as either a wastrel or a threat, a refugee from hard times who'd gone in for pilferage to survive the Panic and found it still to his liking.

They weren't far off, at that; although if they caught on to the whole truth, they might have relented, as Black Bart was known to prick the sides only of Wells and Fargo, who were wealthy men and could afford to bleed a bit; but the same road was traveled by vipers who wriggled their way into a Good Samaritan's home and cut his throat for the contents of his house. Bolton couldn't take the chance of dropping his guard and leaving anyone with an accurate description of Black Bart. He'd come close to that once before and, as with the Strawberry attempt, he learned from his mistakes.

Should he happen to forget, he could thank George W. Hackett for leaving him with a reminder that throbbed like hell's own furnaces every time the fog rolled in from the bay.

On the top shelf of the wardrobe in his bedroom in the Webb House, inside the Montgomery Ward box his boots had come in, were rows of banknotes in neat stacks, hedged in round the edges by sacks of gold coins. (Mattresses were too well-known as caches, and the shelf was too high for the old Chinese woman who brought him hot water and cleaned the room to reach.) He hoisted it down carefully, balancing it to avoid straining his back; it was as heavy as a portable sewing machine.

He dragged his valise from under the bed, opened it on the coverlet, took out the tired old blanket roll, and laid it aside, the hatchet, shotgun, and other tools inside clanking against one another as they shifted. He packed carefully, lining the bottom with stacks of paper currency and placing his clothes on top and tucking a sack of coins between rolled socks. He put several denominations of banknotes in his wallet and tucked some larger bills under the insoles of his dress boots; his hiking pair, worn round now at the heels, the leather cracked from soaking in the rain and drying next to open fires, lay under the bed. He left the rest of the sacks of coins inside the box and returned it to the shelf, placing the blanket roll on top.

Sitting on the bed, he sorted through the maps and stage schedules in the drawer of the nightstand until he came to a railroad timetable. He took it out and studied it, circling various departures with his carpenter's pencil and swigging from his pocket flask until it was empty. Then he undressed, put out the lamp, and slid under the covers, folding his hands behind his head—swimming now; he would never develop resistance to inebriation—and gazing at the papered ceiling the same way he'd hunted constellations in the night sky.

It was as good a time as any for a holiday; and long past time Charles E. Bolton went home.

# FIFTEEN

*The sparrow, they say, finds its way to the nest;*
*and the sun in its turn makes its bed in the west.*
*So Black Bart, "the Po8," and Jim Hume, the sleuth;*
*took rest to prepare for their moment of truth.*

There is no room to bargain, Jim. Your department will function without you present."

Hume looked about him, at the bright silver and crisp linen, the waiters in livery embroidering their way between tables with trays aloft, heard the tinkling of utensils and clicking of crockery, the strings playing on the discreet platform in the corner—"Jeanie with the Light Brown Hair," though it may as well have been "The Wells, Fargo Line"—and grasped the reason for John Valentine's choice for luncheon. Leave it to the tight-fisted general superintendent to select a venue where his guest would not make a scene when told he was being sacked. Carefully he tilted his cigar into a shallow tray and rolled out the burning end. He kept his voice low.

"You should have told me you were releasing me before

we ordered. Now I'll be remembered as the detective who robbed the Company on his way out the door."

Valentine kept his composure. "No one is being released; except you of your responsibilities, for a month. You're not a machine. If I were to allow you to go on as you have without a holiday, I should be an accomplice to suicide."

"I wasn't aware that my health was any concern of the Company's. Or its business, for that matter."

"Be reasonable, Jim. What use are you to Wells and Fargo if you collapse at your desk?"

"Have I given you any reason to think I'm incapable of doing my work? If that's the case, fire me outright."

"You've put more bandits behind bars, and recovered more money, than all your predecessors combined. The Company could do without me more than it could without you, although I'll thank you if that stays at this table. There are other concerns besides Black Bart. You've fixed on him at peril to your well-being."

"My health again. Have I lost weight? Am I pale? Coughing up blood?"

The other sat back, relieving the edge of the table of the pressure of his stomach. "Reach into your inside breast pocket and take out what you find. If it's a handkerchief and not a flour sack with blood on it, I won't press the issue further."

A streak of red scored Hume's cheeks, then faded. "It's nothing. A string tied round my finger, to prevent me from forgetting."

"Untie it. Forgetting about Bart is the point of this conversation. Go back East, visit family."

"I have none."

"Then go north and shoot elk. Let your beard grow. There will still be bandits when you come back."

"Was this your idea?"

"You've told me often enough I have no imagination. It comes directly from Mr. Wells and Mr. Fargo, and will not be withdrawn."

His companion was interrupted in what he was about to say by the waiter, who removed the lid from his tray, set out their meals—slices of rare duck, scalloped potatoes, and asparagus in Hollandaise for Valentine, bread and consommé for Hume's nervous stomach—and refilled their glasses from a pitcher of water.

"Suppose I resign," Hume said when they were alone again. "What then?"

Valentine, tucking his napkin under his collar, chortled. "You won't do that, Jim."

"I won't?"

"You won't. You'd never forgive yourself if someone else takes Black Bart after you left."

"What if it happens while I'm out shooting elk?"

"Then you can come back, shave, and take credit. You've brought us closer to him than anyone else. I'll fire the rascal who follows the tracks you laid to the end and tries to claim the honor."

So it happened that James B. Hume took his first leave of absence in all the years he'd worked for others.

The basement of the brick building, in addition to the safe, a two-ton Acme, black with gilt lettering, bolted to the concrete floor and as ugly as a rich man's daughter, contained the best-stocked arsenal west of Harpers Ferry. Rows of revolvers, shotguns, rifles, carbines, and knives of all sizes occupied locked cabinets glazed in two-inch-thick panes embedded with steel grids, with ammunition in drawers labeled like those that held bolts, screws, and washers in a hardware store. The air was so pungent with oil and polished hickory as to seem slippery to the touch. The clerk in charge, an armorer in everything but name, spent all his time maintaining the inventory. His nails were broken, stained with bluing; the very skin of his face was gunmetal-colored, as if the weapons in his charge had leeched it of flesh and blood. His dundrearies were the shimmery black of black powder, dry to the point of percussion, and his eyes were as balls of lead bright from the crucible. The counter he stood behind, which doubled as a bench, supported a vise in which was clenched the frame of a revolver—a skeletal hand pointing its index finger—with screws, springs, and other components scattered about like pieces of broken toys.

The visitor was a stranger to the clerk, who asked to see his badge and commission papers. When he read the name, his body, slumped upon first contact in the attitude of a craftsman interrupted in his work, came to a sort of attention.

"Ah, yes, Mr. Hume. We don't see you here often."

"Almost never. I do my stalking on the second floor."

The clerk took him on a tour. Given the stature of his guest, he was demonstrably proud of the inventory in his trust, and lingered over items of unique interest; but only to him. Hume hastened him through the exhibition.

"Let me see that one. No, the second to the left."

The clerk wore a ring the size of a cantaloupe chained to his belt. A brass key from the collection unlocked the cabinet. He slid a slim rifle from the rack. "Stevens; the sporting model, chambered for a twenty-two-caliber cartridge. A bit on the light side for elk, Mr. Hume."

The detective made no response. John Valentine, for all his virtues, was a gossip. No doubt a folksy account of the legendary chief of detective's forthcoming rustication would appear in all the evening papers.

He inspected the weapon for balance and heft, approving of its lightness: At fifty-five years of age, more accustomed to riding a Jefferson swivel than a saddle horse, his days of lugging heavy equipment into the wilderness had drawn to a close. He opened and shut the breech, pronounced the action smooth, reversed ends to peer inside the barrel. It was clean, gleaming with a thin application of oil. He switched ends again, shouldered the butt, lined up the sights, and dry-fired the trigger, slinging an imaginary round into the center of the gilt laurels on the door of the safe. Finally he swung the butt to the floor. All these things he did with Marine precision, one of the indelible lessons learned sheriffing. "I'll take a box of shells."

A drawer was unlocked, a deal box produced, and they returned to the clerk's station, where the visitor leaned the rifle against the counter and signed the ledger under the line where a shotgun messenger had made his mark.

"Good hunting, Mr. Hume."

"Thank you. If I come back empty-handed, it won't be the fault of the weapon. I'm not that kind of carpenter who blames his tools."

He had no intention of hunting elk, even if he enjoyed the sport or had a taste for venison; and not just because Valentine had pulled the suggestion out of the air and expected him to follow up on it. Hume deeply resented having been put out to pasture, even if the situation was temporary; which he suspected may not be the case. The division he commanded was filled with ambitious whelps who, entrusted on loan with his responsibilities, would spend every day of his absence undermining him, with the object of making his position theirs; such was the risk inherent in hiring clever men. But the superintendent had underestimated him, thinking that by depriving him of his desk and files he could force him to leisure; forgetting that he had spent years on horseback, crossing and recrossing a county as large as some states in pursuit of outlaws.

Not that his backside welcomed its first contact with a saddle in many months. The roan he drew from the Company stables was sufficiently muscled to negotiate the broken terrain of the Mother Lode, which made it as easy on Hume's own thighs and haunches as straddling a cord of wood; one that was always in motion. He faced the fact that he wasn't the man he'd been when he'd ridden that country in quest for gold; but then that sprout wasn't the man he was now.

Wells, Fargo's chief of detectives did not take holidays.

Like those veterans of the Rebellion who made it a practice to revisit the battlefields where they'd exchanged fire with the enemy, he stopped at most of the scenes of Black Bart's robberies. Some he'd seen before, in company with Sheriff Thorn and others, but many were familiar to him only in the reports that had filled his cabinets, forcing older portfolios into storage in the Montgomery Street basement; he had a clerk's horror of destroying even those documents that predated his appointment to the Company. With the exception of the single foray into Oregon, which he did not trouble to investigate on this trip, they had all taken place within twenty square miles of one another.

Several times he came near his old prospecting attempts, but didn't bother to go even a few hundred yards out of his way to relive that past. It had become so remote it might have belonged to someone else's experience. He slept in the open, and when it rained—with the explosive suddenness of everything else that took place in that country of mountainous trees and lush growth, including sunrise and sunset—he made a tent of the canvas covering his bedroll, supporting it with tree branches and sheltering his upper half. In the morning he awoke soaked to his knees. He hung his stockings on limbs, rolled up his cuffs, and kindled a fire to dry out his boots, which smoked and cracked as surely as Bart's must have time and again. (Hume had not overlooked canvassing all the haberdasheries and booteries in San Francisco and its neighbors, hoping to make contact with someone who remembered selling a particularly stout pair to a customer whose description he might furnish, but it appeared that his quarry had either put as many miles between his home and his sources or ordered by mail.)

Now and again he came across a discarded peach pit or apple core, brown and crawling with ants, and the sensation that Bart had nourished himself on these was so strong he began to believe in fortune-tellers. His man seemed to live mainly off the land, like Napoleon's armies.

Hume did the same, supplementing the provisions he'd

packed with snowshoe hare, Canada goose, and squirrels, targets enough for his light rifle, even though he missed nearly as often as he scored. He'd never enjoyed a sterling reputation in sharpshooting circles, in fact pointed with pride to the dearth of gunfire in his career as a peace officer; but whatever skills he'd possessed hadn't improved through neglect.

There wasn't a report of Bart's activities that he hadn't committed to memory. He stopped at the place where one of the trackers had lost the trail, nearly sixty miles from where the investigation had started. The ground was trampled no longer with the confusion of prints that had ended the pursuit, but Hume identified it by a dead poplar blasted and branded by lightning, and across from it a great bowl-shaped depression, filled now with brackish water and reeking of rotted vegetation, where buffalo had wallowed for centuries before hunters had wiped them out. (He insisted on such detail in all reports intended for his eyes.) The legs of the ancient runner of Marathon had had nothing on Bart's.

When he stopped at the spot near Strawberry where Bart had nearly come to his doom, the sensation of personal proximity became overpowering. This most recent atrocity was electric with "the Po8's" presence. Bedding down, Hume drew out the flour-sack mask, stiff with the blood of his bête noire, glanced around himself guiltily, and drew it over his head. It retained an essence of the grain that had come with it, and also a faint scent of salt-and-iodine: Bart's life-force; it was a wonder there was no trace of brimstone. It was almost like standing face-to-face with his prey, and his pulse quickened.

He awoke hours later with a sense of suffocation. He'd
fallen asleep still wearing the hood. It had been a clear night,
the stars in that high country within groping distance, and
he'd slept exposed to them. Had anyone come upon him,
helpless and wearing this emblem of villainy, he might have
been shot dead where he lay. Sheepishly he snatched it off
and stuffed it back into his pocket.

Two things of miraculous property took place within the
next twelve hours.

As he was leading his horse away from the site of Bart's
encounter with the shotgun messenger, his toe caught something on the ground and he stooped to pick up what he
thought was a scrap of brown wrapping-paper. It was a
man's handkerchief, made of fine lawn linen, soiled with
the mud from several rains and stained with something
more sinister.

Once again his heart thudded. He had no doubt that it
was Bart's own, which he'd used to stop his bleeding. It was
nearly a mile away from the attempted robbery, and must
have been where he'd stopped his flight; it was only by native luck that Hume had quite literally stumbled upon such
promising evidence. He rubbed the corners with a thumb,
scraping away dirt and crusted blood, and found what he'd
hoped for—faded almost to invisibility, but there beyond
doubt. He gave up trying to make it out in the unfavorable
circumstances of that wilderness, then folded it carefully
and tucked it among the other valuables in his wallet.

At dusk, worn thin by the journey and the excitement of
his discovery, he spotted a light in a cabin and stopped to ask
for a berth for the night; his aging bones were begging for
a tick mattress and a proper roof over his head. The man

who opened the door—a man near his age, and a prospector, from the condition of his overalls—peered at him for a long moment, then broke into a welcoming grin.

"You're back!" he said. "I thought you'd be many miles away by now. It's been months!"

James B. Hume had never laid eyes on the man before; and by the time the man realized he was mistaken in his identity, the second miracle was as a thing confirmed.

# SIXTEEN

*The Chinese strike off on a thousand-mile trek;*
*and sailors cross seas at the risk of a wreck.*
*But those who are curs'd with the craving to roam*
*know the longest of tramps is the great journey home.*

He'd traveled by ship, train, and horse, but the experience was so far removed from the present it seemed as much a figment of fancy as the universal dream of flying by the flapping of one's own arms. His jaw ached from clenching, and his buttocks too, from gripping the edge of the seat in the Pullman car. When the train stopped to take on more doomed souls he had to pry his fingers from the padded armrest; it was a marvel they weren't burst and bleeding round the nails.

Stopping was the worst.

A man continued moving forward when the Westing-house brakes were applied—continued moving with a sickening lurch—and it took little imagination to predict what would happen if some force from outside compelled the locomotive to come to a sudden halt; bodies flying from as far back as the caboose to as far forward as the tender, where faces met cast iron at the rate of forty miles per hour.

Then the train started up again.

Starting was the worst.

The cars might have been connected with India rubber bands, so that each was jerked forward uneven to the others, leaving a man's inwards behind him in the next coach down. If another train using the same tracks overran its schedule and slammed into the back of this one—which happened, if the journals could be relied upon, on an almost daily basis—he would race his own entrails, smash through the caboose's rear door, and go tumbling back along the cinderbed, end over end, the ties flaying him alive.

This was how it would be all the way to Des Moines.

He made it as far as Cheyenne, Wyoming Territory.

In that dusty hamlet, stinking of cowshit and green whiskey, he alighted. On the platform, a seated Indian wrapped in a dirty blanket, a soft black hat with a tall crown and a wide brim screwed down to his eyes, a feather stuck in the band, looked him up and down, but before he could scramble to his feet to ask for a handout from the neatly dressed traveler carrying a valise, Bolton had hurried past, wobbling on his land legs and intent on his mission.

He entered a saddlery, heavily scented with leather and bright with sunshine shoving its way through the plate-glass window. The clerk, a man a few years his junior, wearing smoked glasses against the glare, showed him to the racks of boots. Declining an offer to help, he tried on the only pair he could find in his size with heels he didn't fear would topple him onto his face, put his dress pair in the valise, and paid for them with a note that emptied out the clerk's cash box for change. From there the visitor went to a mercantile, where he bought tins of beets, apricots, and tomatoes, and jerked beef in a twist of greasy paper. A dry goods next, for a stiff pair of overalls, four flannel shirts, and four pairs of thick socks, into which the proprietor allowed him the use of his storeroom to change.

His last stop was a pump in the town square, where he filled his canteen, then struck off east, with a sense of freedom and personal control that made him lightheaded and caused him to sing:

> *And there was still another*
> *who well did play his part.*
> *He's known among the mountains*
> *as the highwayman, Black Bart.*
> *He'd walk those mountain passes,*
> *to him it was but pleasure.*
> *He'd hike the trail both night and day*
> *for the Wells and Fargo treasure.*

No law forestalled a man from contributing to a popular air; not that laws proved a barricade to one such as he. Should it make its way onto the circuit where such things flourished, no one but him would know that it was Bart's last fling at rhyme.

The liberty of exploring new territory was as inebriating as strong drink, without the unpleasant aftermath. Here on the plains, the Scourge of the Company was no more than a legend, dismissed as easily as the fabulous adventures of Locksley, Turpin, and Rob Roy; there was none but would suspect a weary passer-through of anything worse than a plea for a night's lodging, and possibly a hot meal, paid for with an amusing anecdote from his passage through history, and when there was no way around it, some chopping of wood. Many a soddy or bunkhouse would carry the memory of the personable chap who graced it with his brief presence, and few to fill the columns of the *Dime Library* with a fresh tale of Black Bart. In such manner he dined on simple but satisfying fare: flapjacks and honey, fritters, fried potatoes and onions, rashers of side pork, and gallons of coffee, piping hot and strong enough to float a stove lid. He slept on feather mattresses, bare springs, straw, and rope hammocks, left only footprints, and took only glad tidings.

Winter came in Nebraska; where winter came with the wrath of Jupiter, piling snow as high as a man's hat against barn sidings and drift fences, coming not down but across, as if a string of boxcars filled with the stuff had stopped long enough to slide the doors open on both sides and let the wind blow bitter flakes across a landscape as flat as a griddle, the icy crystals stinging exposed skin like a plague of yellow jackets and turning fingers and toes into things dead as dominoes.

On the north bank of the Platte, having seen not so much as a stick of civilization in twenty miles, he wrapped himself in two sets of Union suits, duster, blanket, and Chesterfield coat, stuffed with everything pliant from among the smallclothes in his valise, wrapped his head round with one of his flannel shirts after the fashion of a man suffering from an impacted tooth, jammed his bowler down to his ears, dragged his collar up to the brim, and put himself to sleep with the chattering of his teeth on the lee side of a cottonwood as broad in the trunk as a medieval oak from his English birthplace, but not much more shelter than a corn rick. He awoke once during the night to find that the snow had drifted on top of him deep enough to make his supine form indistinguishable from a frozen steer or a ferry run aground; but although disturbed by the possibility of suffocation, he troubled not to shake himself free, clearing only a space to breathe through, so much insulation from the outer-space cold as the snow provided. He'd read somewhere that sled dogs in Alaska burrowed themselves into such drifts in order to survive till morning. Surely he was as intelligent as a dumb brute.

He survived, this night and all the others that followed, or our story would come to an end here.

And he made no complaint, either aloud or in thought. He was made of sterner stuff than that.

As much as he loved the social life of San Francisco, abuzz with cultured conversation, sweet with the odor of roasted brisket, poached salmon, good cigars, and French perfume, entranced with the trills of Italian tenors and Swedish Nightingales, and alive with cable cars chiming their way up and down Telegraph Hill; warmed upon occasion with close contact with pliable women, Charles E. Bolton was a man who throve on challenge, whether it be from man or the elements.

But not beasts.

He shunned all things four-legged. When in bustling Omaha a parti-colored entertainer connected with a medicine show sashayed down the boardwalk, driving before him with a bamboo stick a black bear draped in green-and-yellow motley and brass bells, he crossed to the other side. In his prospecting days he'd come within audible distance of a grizzly panting its powerful way up a heap of slag perpendicular to him, not so far upwind he failed to catch its sweaty, suety stench, redolent of the creatures it had devoured raw. He took refuge in the shaft he'd dug with brother Davy, not venturing out until he was sure the thing was miles distant. For weeks afterward he'd scanned the landscape for its bulky shape before returning to his digs.

Something about the way this trained beast lifted itself onto its hind legs, bawling, in a grotesque parody of a child learning to walk, chilled him to the spine. Better to face a hundred James B. Humes than one bruin, however debased by human trappings. To him, horses, bears, pumas, and the dragons of myth were symbols of terror. Betting on one horse against its peers was as close as he ever cared to come to their savage world; he never placed a wager without hoping one would tumble, shatter a canon, and cause itself to be shot to death in full view of the spectators. His father had not known what he'd wrought when he read Gulliver's *Voyage to the Country of the Houyhnhnms* aloud to him in his infant bed. His terror, no doubt, had contributed to the obstreperous nature of the pack animals he'd been forced to make use of in the goldfields; they were sentient things, and crueler than Herod when they detected weakness. The image of a civilization commanded by the unfeeling creatures still visited him in nightmares.

He'd been making steady progress for four hundred miles, but shortly after crossing the Iowa state line, he became suddenly reluctant to set off on the last short leg of his odyssey, and put up in Council Bluffs for a week. He took lodging in a boardinghouse run by the widow of a railroad baron who'd died of apoplexy less than a month after building the crazy-quilt mansion of turrets, gables, bow-windows, and spires on a hill overlooking the city. She'd spent everything he'd left, realizing belatedly that most of it had gone into the construction (and incidentally the pockets of the general contractor and his cronies), and now eked out her existence letting rooms to strangers and feeding them with the aid of her Negro cook. Her litany of misfortune was the chief topic of conversation during most meals, and stewed tomatoes the feature on the board. He could put up with his hostess' personal tragedy, but loathed the slimy consistency of the dish; however, he made no remark that might draw negative attention. He spent his days reading in his room (novels exclusively; his taste for poetry had tapered off to a great extent) or exploring the streets, retired early most nights, and whiled away one evening in the local opera house watching an uninspired selection from Shakespeare performed by indifferent actors recruited from the community. He missed the cosmopolitan pleasures of San Francisco. It occurred to him then that he was homesick, despite the fact that he'd set out from there to return to the place most would call home.

He left early one morning, while the rest of the household was in bed; all but the cook, who seemed to subsist on two hours' sleep after supervising the girl who washed the dishes and cleaned the kitchen and before rising to prepare breakfast. If she took notice at all of the boarder walking past the open door, dressed for hiking and carrying his valise, she didn't acknowledge him, and went on seasoning her skillets.

The farming village of New Oregon struck him as smaller than he remembered. When he'd settled there, his experience of great, brawling centers of population had been limited to St. Louis and New York City, and the memories of those places blurred behind the fog of war. Even San Francisco had been little more than a rough mining camp when he'd left it the second time. His intimacy with the metropolis it had become made the prospect of a life confined to two stores and a stable surrounded by furrowed acres depressing. Such people as he encountered looked as if they'd been left out in the weather, the men's faces faded to match their homespun shirts, their dungarees blown out in the knees, the women's plain dresses hanging like sandwich boards from their bony shoulders. There was no life in their faces. The thought that he might have remained until he was like them, praying for merciful weather—praying out of habit, not hope—and socializing once a month around a potbelly stove in Wilson's General Merchandise, softened any regret he'd felt for abandoning his family responsibilities and answering the siren call of California. There, it had been easy to think of that chapter in his life as something from a book he'd tried to pound into the goat brains of students in Sierra and Contra Costa counties before that life, too, had palled.

But while a man could run away from such things, half a continent was not far enough. Either it would come after him, peeping under bridges and scouring every house and barn, or he would go looking for it himself; and from himself he could not hide.

He stopped before the place where he'd lived for two

years, and the shame of his leaving struck him like a dash of ice water in the face. The house was a squat single story with a cratered slant roof and the siding rubbed down to gray clapboard, with not a flake of color left to tell a stranger what shade it had been painted.

Pale yellow, he recalled, with blue trim; Wilson's had been overstocked with those at the time, and every third house in the area had sported one or the other or both; the others he'd passed on this trip had all been redone in conventional white. This one bore no sign of a fresh coat in many years. Behind it and to the side, a barn constructed along identical lines still showed traces of red, the traditional rusty hue caused by iron oxide in the paint.

A rail fence separated the burnt-out front yard from the road, the gate hanging at a steep angle from a single strap hinge. He vaguely recalled cutting it from a piece of harness and nailing it in place. ("What good is a fence, Charlie, without a proper gate?") He reached for the top rail, withdrew his hand, then grasped it and eased it open. He remembered a row of flagstones leading to the front porch, sunken now and covered with hardpack earth, if they were still there. The porch roof was swaybacked, and a corner post leaned out forty-five degrees. The boards were spongy underfoot. Something stirred underneath when he stepped up off the ground.

The door, vertical planks reinforced with two more describing an X, was locked, to his surprise. It had had only a latch and string when he'd lived there. An iron plate had been added, with a keyhole into which he could fit his little finger.

He set down his valise, stepped to the end of the porch that was still supported by a relatively straight timber, leaned against a dirty, sun-bleached window, rubbed a hole in the grime, and leaned against the pane, cupping his hands around his eyes. When they adjusted to the gloom inside, watered down by sunlight poking through the holes in the roof, he looked at a bare iron bedstead sagging drunkenly toward a missing leg, a rocking chair with its upholstery in tatters, broken crates, and piles of rubbish, here and there shredded and balled into nests by creatures to which a locked door presented no obstacle. A lithograph print of George Washington's farewell address to his troops hung crooked in its pasteboard frame on the wall next to a chipped enamel wash basin. He remembered the print vaguely; it had been part of a set, with the Delaware crossing and Valley Forge hung alongside. All these things would be steeped in a stench of mold, rodent droppings, and dry rot; the fetor not of defilement, but of neglect.

The house might have gaped empty for half a century instead of the decade and a half he'd been gone; or more likely less. Lizzie and the girls would have hung on until hope, too, deserted them. In even the happiest of homes, life on the plains was like a dog's, aging seven to the year. *Had* the home been happy, even for a little while? He couldn't remember.

The daughters should be married now, if diphtheria or consumption or cholera or scarlet fever hadn't intervened, or any of the myriad other evils that threatened youth and age indiscriminately. These horrors had helped to make of him a coward where the full force of the Confederacy could not, and driven him, as decisively as George W. Hackett's lead slug, into flight. If it was marriage, Lizzie may have gone to live with one of her new families. If it was death, the ghosts alone would have driven her away.

He made no attempt to enter, but retrieved his valise and tramped back into town. One thing had been added in his absence: In Wilson's store, where pipes, tinned tobacco, and gentlemen's watches had been on display (and had attracted more dust than attention), a lady's dress shop shared the floor, with a row of frocks hanging from a pipe rack, four shelves of gingham and calico in bolts, and a square table where a young woman with freckles the size of dimes stood cutting fabric with a large pair of shears.

"Boles?" she replied to his query; and turned toward a thick-waisted woman of forty draping scraps of material on a dress form on an iron pedestal, a thing of curved and jointed plates like medieval armor. "Boles?"

The older woman turned her head to peer at the visitor through rimless spectacles. "The widow?"

His heart fell. Yes, that was the story Lizzie would put about to forestall inconvenient conversation; or how she may in fact think of herself. He nodded.

"Gone." She busied herself again with her swatches.

"Where?"

"Where do they all go? Back East."

"And the daughters?"

She turned her head again, not quite far enough to meet his gaze: Shrugged.

He went back outside. He'd heard it said that members of small communities fettered themselves in the close bonds of Christian brotherhood. He had never known such to be the case in practice.

He reached in the pocket where he'd placed a folded
sheaf of notes—an amount sufficient to support a family of
average size for a year—and put them back in his wallet.
Then Charles E. Bolton, né Boles, more lately Black Bart,
turned and began retracing his steps toward the Pacific.

# SEVENTEEN

*Now, a bird with a sprinkle of salt can be caught,*
*and a fly with molasses its fate can be bought.*
*Though a man is the craftiest creature of all,*
*the smallest of trifles can bring on his fall.*

Despite Wells, Fargo's reputation for privacy and discretion, Jim Hume would sooner place his secrets in the hands of a ladies' sewing circle. Everyone he encountered, from the brass buttons who opened the door for him to the hardworking Jon Thacker when he entered his office, greeted him with the same question:

"Did you get your elk?"

And Hume provided the same answer:

"I believe I have."

He was lean and tanned, his freshly barbered hair and moustaches bleached white against the brown of his face, and he walked at a brisk clip, throwing this remark over his shoulder as he went straight to his station. Halfway there he stopped.

"Who in God's name plundered my desk?"

He'd thought at first that someone, acting out of some notion of benevolent reward, had replaced the item of furniture with a newer, sleeker model. It had been so long since he'd seen its top, leather stretched like the skin on a drum and fixed with bronze tacks around the edges, that he failed to recognize the pilot's bridge from which he'd directed the Company's security operations for more than ten years.

His secretary leapt from his chair. "I did, sir; at Mr. Valentine's direction. He thought your, er, substitute—"

"Replacement, you mean. Has this new arrangement brought him any closer to Black Bart?"

"No, sir, but he—that is, Mr. Valentine—"

"You can tell Mr. Valentine—no, I'll tell him myself directly. When I return, I want everything back as it was, in the order in which I left it." His indignation ebbed in the presence of his assistant's blanched face; in point of fact, his elation over the discovery he'd made during his "holiday" would not bear anger of any duration. He smiled thinly, the equivalent in him of a barn-door grin. "As near as you can come; there's a good fellow. My pack rat system isn't pretty, but it has method."

The superintendent beamed at him from behind his own desk. "You're brown as a nut, Jim. Did you get your elk?"

"A trophy buck." He took the soiled handkerchief from his pocket, held it up by the corners, and let it unfurl like bunting.

"Well?" he said, when Valentine made no remark.

"I'm waiting for you to produce a white dove from the folds."

"Give me a week at the outside and I shall."

"I am all ears."

"You are aware of the fact that professional laundries advertise their services by staining the items they clean with the name of the establishment in some unobtrusive spot, or a symbol unique to it, in India ink?"

"I am. I am also aware that the earth revolves from west to east, and that my wife is incapable of leaving her dressmaker's without spending at least fifty dollars. Is Wells, Fargo going into the laundry business now? I must check my mail more often."

"I am, if it is not. See for yourself."

Valentine took the proffered item and peered at the corner his chief of detectives had indicated with a finger. He slid open the belly drawer of his desk, excavated a brass-framed magnifying lens with a bamboo handle from the clutter inside—unlike Hume, the superintendent preferred to keep the day's detritus out of sight—and studied the smudge of ink through the glass, oscillating it between his eye and the square of dirty linen until the edges sharpened. It was a row of letters followed by a numeral:

$$F.X.O.7.$$

"I can't make out the meaning. Why must they use a code? I thought the whole point was to advertise the establishment."

"I shall ask the proprietor when I make his acquaintance."

"You think this belongs to Black Bart?"

"It belongs to us now." He related the circumstances of its discovery. "There is blood on it. In his distress after being wounded, he became careless and left it behind."

Valentine deposited the handkerchief on his desk; scowled at the filthy thing upsetting the tidy symmetry of his arrangements, scooped it up, and returned it to Hume. "I find it difficult to raise a ruckus over a souvenir. Place it with your peach pits, apple cores, and whatnot, and we'll put it on display when we have our man."

Hume kept his patience. Expecting his superior to have developed an imagination in his absence was feckless.

"Peach pits can't be traced. I intend to show it to every laundry in town."

"My God, man, this is San Francisco! There must be a hundred—"

"Ninety-one, to be exact. I stopped at City Hall on the way here and spent an hour in the records office."

"Too thin, Jim. No law forbids a man from tending his injury. Even if you succeed in tracing that rag to Bart, it won't prove he committed a robbery, let alone—what's the tally, now? I disremember."

"Twenty-five, if we accept Little Lake. Thacker has informed me of the Redding and Cloverdale runs. Bart seems to have been eager to make up for time lost while he recovered from Strawberry." He folded the handkerchief along its creases, returned it to his pocket, and patted it. "We'll worry about tying Bart to his wicked deeds once we have him in manacles. Unless he's been spending like Ben Thorn, he's stashed the money somewhere he can get to it; and so can we."

"Tell me, Jim, did you spend any part of your holiday not on Company business?"

"I smoked a couple of dozen cigars."

\*　\*　\*

The chief had wearied of conducting an on-foot investigation. Bart's peripatetic ways did not suit him. He was more comfortable seated at his desk, letting his eyes wander through reams of written reports; his sojourn in City Hall's dusty cellar, studying the list of licenses assigned to laundering establishments, had been a pleasant return to his normal habits. Matching the cryptic mark to its place of origin, however, required a different kind of patience, one in which only one man in his experience excelled all others.

On reputation alone, Harry Morse had seemed everything that Jim Hume and John Valentine wished to avoid in associating a man with the Company. At the age of forty-two, he'd served Alameda County as sheriff for fourteen years, during which he'd collected adventures enough to crimson the paper covers of any of the sensational publications that poured off the eastern presses like entrails from a belly wound. When he took office, a blight of Mexican bandits had terrorized the jurisdiction for years, in numbers to rival the pirates of the old Spanish Main. By the time he was offered a post with Wells, Fargo, they were few and in constant flight.

In a later day, critics would excoriate the lawman for persecuting a particular group while ignoring white felons. Hume knew not if Morse held any personal distaste for Mexicans; he seemed simply to have broken the code of behavior peculiar to criminals from that stratum of society. He'd slain Narrato Ponce, a cattle rustler and killer, after a long chase on lathered mounts through the spires of Pinole Canyon, with a single rifle ball fired from a pitching saddle. Jesus Tejada slaughtered five people in a store for a treasure that amounted to forty dollars American, but when he found out who was pursuing him for the atrocity, surrendered himself without resistance. Narcisco Bojorques paralyzed the population for months, leaving his mark on his victims by driving a stake through their skulls, until a round from Morse's pistol found him.

"That one doesn't count," the sheriff had told a reporter. "I only winged him. Someone else put a bullet through his heart in a saloon over a disagreement of some kind. A wizard bit of marksmanship, given the size of the target."

"Is it true you're the man who killed Joaquin Murieta?" asked the disappointed journalist.

"It was not Joaquin. If that's his head in a jar in Frisco, I never saw it in life. I merely killed the man who committed most of the murders that were assigned to him."

Perhaps it was this remark, widely quoted, that had decided Hume to invite the man to Montgomery Street back in 1876: It combined a lack of swagger with a passion for accuracy, two things the detective chief held dear.

He made a favorable impression from the start. Instead of the long-haired dandy that journalists expected of a blood-and-thunder gunman, a clean-shaven Irishman with bright eyes and a wide, humorous mouth stepped into the office, carefully barbered and wearing a collar as stiff and white as a plumb line in chalk. He looked several years younger than he was, and except for the yellow bone handle belonging to a long-barreled Colt that revealed itself when he spread his tails and sat down, his tailoring would not excite comment in the lobby of the Palace Hotel.

Hume had asked him about none of his exploits; he'd read all the accounts, adjusted them to allow for newspaper fuddle, and framed his questions to determine whether the man possessed any detecting skills. The answers impressed him, and he hired him, just as Valentine (who for all his plodding intelligence was at least a shrewd judge of character) had appointed Hume. Both the chief and this new recruit were modest to the point of irritation when offered a compliment.

Now, seven years later, Special Agent Morse showed few of the signs of aging that had thinned Hume's temples and scored lines in his brow since Black Bart had come to his attention. A solid record of accomplishments and a true passion for his work had managed to preserve that first impression of a merry son of Erin.

"Good morning, Harry. It was good of you to come so promptly." Hume rose to grasp the hand offered by his visitor, a thing strung with wire and calloused as thickly as a canvas glove.

Harry Morse smiled and took his old seat.

"Wild horses couldn't keep me away once I saw Black Bart's name in your wire."

The desk between them (after some adjusting by its owner) had returned to its customary condition of dishevelment. Atop the stack was the badly used handkerchief, forming a sort of tent.

The detective chief snatched up the handkerchief and tossed it into Morse's lap. "This is the first solid clue to his identity we've come up with. I found it myself by pure chance; and his description the same way." He related the details of his overnight stay in the very cabin where Bart had spent a night, adding uncomfortably, "Evidently he and I share some common physical characteristics."

Morse, studying the item, made no comment. Whether the cause was discretion or professional preoccupation, Hume was grateful.

"It's not the golden key, not yet," he said. "It will take a great deal of legwork before anything comes of it; but you're used to that. At the very least it's an opportunity to get all your cleaning done at the expense of the Company."

The special agent stood and pocketed the handkerchief. "I'm out of luck as always. I just had mine done."

# III

# BALLAD'S END

*A man cannot be too careful in his choice of enemies.*

—Oscar Wilde

# EIGHTEEN

*Bart traveled the Lode with his feet on the ground.*
*He thought by this trick that he'd never be found.*
*'Twas then that one of the men on his trail*
*stepped out of leather and put him in jail.*

The old ways were drawing to a close, casting long shadows toward the east. They were playing stickball on Pacific Street, on stones stained yet with the blood of vigilantes and hoodlums, and Hop John's old opium parlor in Chinatown hosted mah-jongg parties on Saturday night. There were times when one could actually feel the earth throbbing, like a powerful engine inexorably in motion.

*It will take a great deal of legwork before anything comes of it,* Jim Hume had said; *but you're used to that.*

Harry Morse wasn't, though, if one took "legwork" literally. The word was new to him; he suspected it was Hume's own coinage. He'd run down most of his game from horseback, galloping balls-out across the flats and sliding forefoot first down mountainsides smeared with loose shale. But seven years in San Francisco had shown him the future of law enforcement: Equestrianship would play a diminishing role on the cusp of a new century. Residents traveled by cable car and trolleys pulled by docile beasts that had never been whipped up above a trot. A man riding astraddle was getting to be rare enough to attract interest. How long before curiosity gave way to derision?

He himself felt a bitter urge to chuckle at the picture of a mounted lawman carrying a gentleman's handkerchief from one laundry to another, the effete thing flapping like a lady's silk scarf tied round a knight's arm. No, when a robber's fate turned on an item of haberdashery instead of a fast horse and a sure aim, the West was no longer a place for knights.

If in fact it ever had been. He'd spent most of his time as Alameda County Sheriff either frying in the sun or red-ass from constant soakings in the rain, staking out reeking outhouses and whoring parlors where the women's breasts hung like feed sacks and the crabs were as big as snails in a French restaurant.

Still, there had been adventure in it, and no suspicion that what he was about couldn't be managed by a servant with congested lungs. He hadn't signed with the Company in order to plod from one homely sopping-wet establishment to another like some gentleman's gentleman dropping off his master's soiled underdrawers. But for his regard for Hume, Morse would be tempted to put in for a post as a shotgun messenger at a substantial reduction in pay.

At the beginning, the Black Bart affair had appealed to his methods. He'd traced the bandit's route through gold country, stopping in at settlers' homes hoping to prove his theory that even the hardiest of trekkers would seek the comfort of a bed and a ceiling overhead, if only for a night, but had been unable to find anyone who recalled putting up anyone more interesting than a weary middle-aged victim of economic ruin. That had been his cardinal error, to buy into the prevailing assumption that only a young man in full possession of his health would essay such an undertaking; that, on the evidence of Hume's voluminous files, applied to highwaymen in general. He little thought the dusty old derelicts he learned of fitted the mold. Now he understood that most, if not all, of these unfortunates described to him were indeed one man, or took under consideration what now seemed obvious: Cleverness was often a byproduct of years and experience.

As sheriff on the trail of rogue Mexicans, he'd had the advantage of his Irish heritage, and of a shared understanding of revolution against foreign authority. The rebel strain had enabled him to think as they thought, and predict their course. This was the best strategy of the detective, years before he'd applied to himself so top-lofty a title: the ability to crawl inside the mind of a criminal.

Now he was forced to borrow Hume's own tactic of keeping records. Ninety-one laundries made a prodigious list, and led to the necessity of striking off each place he'd visited to avoid retracing old ground. For one of the enterprises was much the same as the rest, whether it was a dreary room in a shared flat where an old woman or a man even older, in pigtails and a filthy mandarin's cap, scrubbed dingy shirts in a galvanized tub and sweated over a red-hot iron, or a production line where a dozen laborers without proof of legal residency stood at mangles in rows, pressing creases into hundreds of sheets and tablecloths delivered on pallets from hotels, hospitals, and restaurants. He developed a lifelong revulsion for the smell of lye soap and cornstarch and hellish humid heat; as well as a decidedly unprofessional pity for those who were forced to spend fourteen hours a day in their presence.

And the list itself was unreliable. On the strength of rumor and applied eavesdropping, he visited at least a dozen venues that operated without a license; most with a hand resting on the butt of his revolver, lest one of the edged weapons typical of the riffraff make its appearance. The city's inspectors were infamous for ferreting out unlawful shops under the guise of a customer or a visitor on some business other than exposure.

Blank faces met his inquiries; that, and native suspicion of an outsider penetrating their society without a bundle under his arm to justify the expenditure of their time. Even the hint of reward for assistance in the extraction of a festering thorn in the Company's side met only suspicion from the Chinese. In the history of Wells, Fargo's practice of offering bounty, not a single resident of Oriental blood had seen a cent.

Once, shortly after leaving behind another dead end, he found himself followed by three Chinese in slop-shop suits and tight-fitting caps, potential Tong highbinders, likely armed with hatchets and daggers. They remained behind him at a distance of twenty yards for three blocks, until he swung aboard a passing trolley. After this encounter, he made certain to prepare himself subsequently with a sack of his own clothing, sometimes supplementing it with perfectly clean items fresh from the business he patronized regularly. Despite Hume's promise, he had no hope of redeeming the expense. The Messrs. Wells and Fargo might lay out a thousand dollars to revenge themselves against the felonious loss of a hundred, but would balk at authorizing six bits for a pristine stack of shirts. Still, it was a cheap enough price to pay to prevent bloodstains in the next bundle.

The places he visited in Chinatown—the likeliest place to begin—did not lack for imagination in the proprietary marks they pressed into their washing. They used initials, numerals, Chinese calligraphy, stylized representations of Buddha, dragons, peacocks, and the single baleful eye of the Freemasons; but none fell remotely close to the F.X.O.7. There was nothing in it to suggest the Far East, but some of the Oriental enterprises were sensitive to the prevailing distrust of the race and adopted something Occidental in appearance.

As with Hume's own discovery of the handkerchief, success came accidentally.

On Stevenson Street, on his way home from another disappointment, he spotted a sign in a window:

**THE CALIFORNIA LAUNDRY**
**P. Ferguson & J. Biggs, props.**

It was a large operation and tidy, with a long paneled counter transecting the room, and beyond it a door—leading, presumably, to the facilities in back—set tightly into its frame so as to prevent corrosive odors from offending customers. The shirt-waisted young woman behind the counter would not commit to an answer, but went through the door, closing it quickly against a cloud of steam, and returned momentarily with a bald-headed man in a gray suit of clothes, who introduced himself as Phineas Ferguson, senior partner in the firm, and asked to see verification of Morse's authority. He studied the shield, then nodded, stretching the handkerchief between his hands.

"Yes, this is our mark."

The special agent fought back a flush. "Is there one here who could identify the owner?"

"No," Ferguson said; and Morse's heart fell. "The *O*, you see, belongs to our branch on Bush Street. Talk to Mr. Ware." He gave him an address.

"And the seven?"

"That would be the number assigned to the customer."

Morse took back the item, conquering the urge to snatch it out of the man's hand. As he turned to go:

"I doubt you'll make it. It closes in five minutes."

It was a bitter setback. To have come so close after having gone down so many blind alleys, only to have to wait till morning, would make for a sleepless night. The noisome thought that his bird would fly came to him only when he was this close and something came between. But detective work, Hume had said, was "nine parts hard work and one part hope." He pushed out into the street and swung aboard a passing trolley. He alighted at Union Square and ran a block, arriving at the address at eight minutes past five o'clock.

Most of the ground-floor frontage belonged to a tobacco shop bearing the name of Thomas Ware; information that did not make him pause. Laundry services were used almost exclusively by men, and enterprising tobacconists often donated part of their square footage to the establishments in order to divert trade from competitors; for while one could scarcely walk three blocks in San Francisco without passing a laundry, he could expect also to find a place to buy cigars and pipe tobacco just a few doors away.

The laundry was entered through a separate door, the top half of which was glazed. Just as he came to it, an amber-hued face as smooth as ancient porcelain (and likely of similar vintage) glared at him through the glass. She was drawing down the paper shade.

Morse took out a fold of banknotes and brushed the edge down the pane.

The hand hesitated, then let go, allowing the shade to snap back up onto its roll with a clatter. A latch snapped. His hand was on the knob when the door swung open, snatching it from his grasp, and the porcelain face thrust itself into the six-inch gap. The tight cap of snow-white hair barely cleared the knob, and he had to reach down to take hold of it.

"We close. Go home." She had seen the bundle under his arm.

"A moment of your time, madam. I'm not here for the cleaning." He separated a note from the fold and held it out. She took it and stretched it between her hands, peering at it against the light from the front window. She turned and circled behind a plain counter, at which station she was emphatically in authority. Threads of steam issued between strings of beads hanging in a doorway at her back.

She wore black bombazine, clutched at her throat by a cameo pin, the essence of western dress; but the ivory in the brooch matched her flesh, and from the neck up she bore a close resemblance to the Dowager Empress; although he suspected this woman was many years her senior. When he unfolded the handkerchief and offered it for her inspection, she stared at it suspiciously, then thrust the note she had crumpled in her fist into a pocket, as if he might try to take it back, took the square of soiled linen, and held it close to her face for a moment. She thrust it back. "No."

"Are you saying it's not your mark, or you don't know whom the handkerchief belongs to?"

"We close. Go!"

But recognition had sparked in her eyes when she was examining the item. The Chinese were no more inscrutable than Mexicans were lazy and stupid.

"Is Mr. Ware in?"

"Go! We close!"

"What seems to be the problem, Mrs. Yee?"

Morse turned to face the owner of the voice, a well-set-up man in his thirties in shirtsleeves, waistcoat, and pince-nez spectacles trailing a green ribbon. Another door hung open behind him, offering a glimpse of a Stonehenge arrangement of deal cigar boxes on a pedestal display. "I am Thomas Ware, the proprietor."

Morse started to reach for his shield, but instinct stopped him. Instead he passed over the handkerchief. If this weren't his last stop, it would soon wear through from handling. "Can you give me the name of the man who owns this?"

Ware studied it. His expression was wary. "What is this in regard to?"

"My name is Harry Hamilton." His own name had appeared in print nearly as often as Jim Hume's. "I met the gentleman briefly, but failed to get his name. He left this behind. It's a fine piece and should be returned to its owner."

The proprietor's face brightened. "Are you a mining man as well?"

# NINETEEN

*Eight years is a spell for a fox to stay loose;*
*but a fox is more sly than a pig or a goose.*
*Still, a hound is its cousin, just under the fur,*
*and eight years or eighty, the finish is sure.*

The Buckley Saloon was furnished elegantly, as befit its location within brief walking distance of busy Union Square. It contained a long mahogany bar equipped with a brass rail, blue-enamel-lined cuspidors conveniently placed, original paintings in crenulated frames of nymphs and satyrs, and a long tilted mirror behind the bar, tinted amethyst to flatter those reflected in it, turning dissipated old sots into distinguished elder statesmen and hard-faced tarts into beauties from the rotogravure. The roseate shade extended to the glass chimneys of Chesterfield lamps suspended from the ceiling. The piano, painted white with blue trim, was unmanned at that hour, its keys covered. A mutton-chopped bartender in a figured waistcoat glowered at the two men taking up a gaming table with no deck in sight—customers who came in just to drink generally stood at the bar—but it was late morning and business was at a trickle, so he held his tongue and applied elbow grease to a sticky spill on the bar with his rag.

They were respectable enough for that establishment: middle-aged men in good linen who didn't demand service as if he were the Negro boy who emptied the cuspidors. And they looked good for a decent gratuity. He wished he could say as much for the moocher laying siege to the complimentary cold cuts on the strength of one beer. He was a regular, dependable as an eight-day clock.

"Broken down to individual customers," said James B. Hume to his companion, examining the laundry mark yet again; it had become a talisman every bit as much as Bart's bloody flour sack. "This Ferguson is a fellow after my own heart. I should take my cleaning there."

Harry Morse toyed with his glass of beer. He looked down and saw he had etched F.X.O.7. in the condensed moisture on the outside. Impatiently he rubbed it out with his thumb.

"You can check the place out yourself," he said. "It's only a few doors down. Since Ferguson and Biggs opened a branch in this neighborhood, the local men have relieved their wives of the chore of dropping off and picking up the laundry."

His superior stopped fingering the handkerchief, dipped the end of his cigar in his rye, and returned it to his lips. The man must have smoked twenty a day; but this was the first time the special agent had seen him drink anything stronger than coffee. The atmosphere round the table was one of cautious celebration.

Hume said, "I'd much rather meet the man. If he's as friendly with this fellow Bolton as you say, he can give us a fair picture of whom to look for. If we approach the wrong man at—What is it again?"

"The Webb House, twenty-seven Post Street."

"A respectable location; but then he can afford it." He pulled a face. "We mustn't chance spooking our quarry. We're not like those blunderers at Pinkerton."

"Fortunately, this one doesn't live with his mother."

"Thank heaven for that."

In 1875, agents with the Pinkerton National Detective Agency had flung an incendiary device into the Jesse James house in Clay County, Missouri, blowing an arm off the bandit's mother and killing his nine-year-old half-brother. Jesse and his brother Frank had been miles away at the time, and the incident had elevated them from murderous bushwhackers to folk heroes. Six long years would elapse, and dozens of robberies committed, before an assassin's bullet brought Jesse's career to an end. The incident served as a cautionary tale for manhunters throughout the nation.

"You're quite sure this man Ware hasn't been in communication with Bolton?"

"I was certain you'd want to be in on the kill, so I followed him home from the laundry and kept watch on his house all night. At dawn I sent a message to Stone and asked him for a man to relieve me while I slept two hours. He's still on duty."

"Good man, Stone." The San Francisco police captain was a longtime Company ally.

Hume downed his drink, drew one last time on his cigar, and mashed it out in a bronze tray. "Let us go talk to Ware, this time with the gloves off."

"No need to rise. That's him, over at the free lunch."

Hume looked at a well-groomed young man standing at the sideboard, loading a plate with shaved ham, oysters from a bowl of chipped ice, and sliced bread, under a hefty odalisque reclining in a frame. The model wore a silk wrap that was not quite opaque enough for his taste.

"I felt there was a reason you chose this place to meet; although you might have told me before I put out my cigar."

Morse suppressed a grin. "I felt you'd approve. About the saloon, I mean."

The former Alameda County Sheriff was accustomed to such venues, although few in those hard-riding years were as opulent. He'd picked hops and other bits less pleasant from green beer served by louts with black nails in flyblown hovels, eavesdropping on conversations that had led him to a string of arrests. Hume, on the other hand, preferred to do his drinking in private, gin-houses being the natural habitat of journalists and dime-novel scribblers.

His companion attracted the attention of a silhouette standing in the shade of the awning outside the front window and made a quick saluting gesture. The officer stirred itself and withdrew. His assignment was ended.

At a nod from Hume, Morse caught the diner's eye and beckoned him over. The laundryman approached, balancing the plate in one hand and gripping a full beer mug with the other. He blinked when he saw Hume, started to smile; then reddened.

"Your pardon, please," he said. "I took you for someone else at first."

The two Wells, Fargo men exchanged a glance. The description the lumberman had provided of the vagabond he'd seen loitering near Berry Creek, and of the stranger who'd overnighted in the prospector's cabin on the road from Strawberry, was confirmed: Hunter and hunted bore a close physical resemblance.

Introductions were made. The detectives watched closely to see if Thomas Ware recognized the name Jim Hume, but he gave no indication. He drew a chair from another gaming table and sat perched on the edge. The bartender's scowl deepened; but he went on dunking glasses in a tub of soapy water and polishing them with a fresh towel.

"Will you forgive me?" Ware asked, glancing down at his plate. "I didn't break my fast this morning."

Hume nodded again, and the newcomer picked up the sandwich he'd built. Morse, having decided to let the chief of detectives do the interrogating, finished his beer and raised his hand to order another.

"You may have mine." Ware slid his glass forward. "I'm not a drinking man. I ask for it only so I can lunch here and make ends meet."

"I should think the manager of any business in this neighborhood wouldn't have to count his pennies," Hume said.

The other flushed again and lowered his voice. "I'm paying penance, I'm afraid. I lost a good bit recently at Ocean View Park."

"You're married, I take it?" Morse smiled.

Ware stared uncomfortably at his sandwich. "Charlie's usually more reliable in his recommendations."

Hume jumped on this. "That would be Charles Bolton, your mining friend?"

"Yes. Please don't think me reckless by nature. I attended

the races with him by invitation, purely for his companionship. I'd never laid so much as a nickel on a hand of cards, and bet only that one time, encouraged by the consistency of his good fortune. The horse came in fourth, by half a length. Then he said a funny thing."

"Not many men would find humor in the situation."

"I should have said queer. 'It serves me well for placing my faith in one of the brutes.' That's what he said."

Again the detectives' gazes locked.

"It served you too," Hume said.

"I said something of the kind. I was upset. Right away he was sympathetic, and apologized for steering me wrong. I really think my loss upset him more than his own. He wouldn't be done with apologizing. I found myself having to console him rather than the other way round."

"He's that pleasant?"

"Indeed. Everyone at work finds him so, including Mrs. Yee; who likes no one."

"Quite the gambler, is he?"

"I wouldn't go so far. He rarely lays down more than two dollars. He assures me he exercises the same restraint at the fights. I take him at his word there. I've never gone myself, although he's asked. Beastly barbaric, that sport. It should be outlawed everywhere."

"I and my wallet agree," put in Morse; and got a fierce look from Hume for the interjection. He raised his glass to his lips, hiding his amusement. Morse had slain mad killers: He didn't find the chief the dragon others did.

Ware, who had taken advantage of Hume's questions to eat, chewing and swallowing rapidly in order to answer them, put down his sandwich. "May I ask the reason for this interest? I should think there's a club or something where you mining men all go."

"There is, although I doubt your Charlie is a member. A wolf in fleece rarely socializes with shepherds. They don't fool as easily as the flock." Hume showed his palm with his shield in it. The laundryman started and looked at the other detective, who held out his own. "Harry Morse. Hamilton is the manufacturer's name engraved on my watch."

# TWENTY

*Much of our tale remains to be told;*
*of Black Bart, Jim Hume, and the struggle for gold.*
*But in late '83, despite Wells, Fargo's rage,*
*the robber and "Po8" took down his last stage.*

He was always reading about inner voices warning a fellow away from a plan; Shakespeare was full of it. But it wasn't a voice, or anything remotely human. Rather it was a kind of buzzing, a droning stirring of wings, as was made by a fly stuck in a screen, with scant hope of freeing itself, but too accustomed to living to give up and wait for oblivion.

The sound was so vivid he looked around for the doomed insect before he realized the vibration was coming from inside him, and that it had begun the moment he came to the top of Funk Hill.

The coach bound from Sonora to Milton would climb that grade; the very spot where he'd struck the Company the first time in July 1875.

Charles Bolton was not a superstitious man, but neither did he pass unknowingly under a ladder lest a bucket of whitewash or a hod of bricks fall on his head, or otherwise tempt fate. Passing through a place where a robbery had once been committed, the coachman would be naturally upon his guard, and if accompanied by an armed messenger, equipped with a hair trigger.

The noise was as persistent as a bout of hiccups, a sneezing jag, a nerve jumping in his cheek; it would not go away. He quit the site to scout out a replacement.

All the other places were unsuitable for one reason or another. One provided too narrow a field of observation, another lacked sufficient cover, a third failed to appeal for no reason he could determine. He returned to the hilltop he associated with Black Bart's christening.

Here, at the crest of a steep incline, the road grew narrow, entering a bootjack turn after what was a long pull for the best of teams; and the Company hung steadfast to its stove-in, hollow-flanked nags along this lonely stretch, with no goal in sight beyond a rubdown with burlap sacks and a nosebag adulterated with acorns; the nefarious stage agents would charge them to the Company as premium oats. A slow coach, and a driver with knots between his shoulders, was like a crippled goose to a hungry hawk. It was why he'd chosen Funk Hill in the first place. Nothing had changed.

The buzz was gone now, and in its place a pang of bittersweet memory.

Waiting behind this same rock, he'd felt his head swim and his heart pound; it seemed that if he didn't fix his eyes on some solid thing—a fir trunk, a pebble, the elf's-hat patch of moss on the crown of the boulder, anything anchored firmly to the earth—his soul would fly away. Many years had passed, and many a shaken driver sent on his way, since he'd felt anything to compare to it; although the hum of anticipation remained, and the elation warming his veins like strong wine in the aftermath.

In the shadow of the rock he spread his blanket, laid aside the hatchet, shotgun, hammer, wrecking bar, and a battered coffeepot and tin cup—innovations, these last, made necessary by rheumatism in the joints—and sat with his back against the cool granite. It was getting on dark; there would be no travelers along this path before morning to spot a suspicious fire. He built one of pine twigs tented with cottonwood branches and prepared a cowboy's blend of grounds thickened slightly with water from his canteen. While it was brewing, he cut wedges with his pocketknife from one of the apples he'd gathered along the way. No frost had yet come in that balmy, old-gold, post-October season, to sweeten the fruit; they were small and shriveled, woody, and the stiff skins stuck in his teeth. Those peaches that remained on this route were nearly past their time, and Mexican picking-crews were harvesting them in numbers that demanded caution from a passing stranger. He washed down the disappointing pulp with coffee—bitter sludge, but piping hot—and hummed "The Wells, Fargo Line," without relish this time. The memory of that macabre buzzing suggested there would not be many more of these idylls. The thrill evaporated before his eyes.

Even the scrap from *The Sacramento Bee* he'd wrapped around a sleeve of crackers consumed during a resting stop, and had saved for reading, contained little of interest in the flickering light, prurient or otherwise. Newspapers were the painted woman of the printed word: intriguing on contact, a disappointment in the consumption. The press had passed him by, aside from brief accounts of the four robberies he'd brought off since the ignominious Strawberry affair; and for the first time in his adopted profession, he felt no slight. Repetition, the absence of colorful and insolent poetry (he'd gone dry, truth to tell; writers' block wasn't the exclusive province of those who made their living from it) had taken away its novelty, for the recorders as well as for the perpetrator. Black Bart was news as old as the Garfield assassination.

When the practice of staking life and limb on an enterprise surrendered its excitement, what was left? His memoirs, perhaps; the last refuge of retired generals and presidents out of office. Which in his case would amount to a confession and loss of liberty.

And the critics would insist upon rhyme.

He could return to teaching school; but he doubted the generation of students that had arisen since his last post offered any more inspiration than the dullards who'd preceded it. Their only ambition was to hear the clanging of a cowbell signifying the end of their torment. Grown men and women, now, propagating their ignorance in their heirs. An idiot, once taught to read, was an idiot still.

Prospecting wasn't in it, even if he possessed the endurance and ambition of youth. At a time when the great mining interests that had driven him from the field—with the assistance of Wells and Fargo—were closing dry shafts and sacking laborers, dreams of wealth and independence went down the road in their wake, to day wages and death in the service of others. Reunite with his family? They had abandoned him as he had them, and well served. He was a bounder and no mistake.

The nattering of birds awoke him in full daylight. His bladder was full. He made water, and was buttoning his fly when came a noise not indigenous to nature: the familiar refrain of rattling tack, churning hooves, and creaking leather straps. Yet another lamb to the slaughter. With the weary resignation of a digger of ditches retrieving his pick and shovel, he bent and lifted his shotgun; not forgetting to draw the flour sack over his head.

\* \* \*

Across Post Street from the unprepossessing façade of the Webb House, Harry Morse paused to roll a cigarette. The officer leaning in the deep doorway belonging to a printing plant remained motionless. The prominent bones of his face caught the light of the flame from Morse's match and he wore his soft hat and mail-order suit as if he put it on every day. It bespoke nothing of the bullet-shaped helmet and stiff serge uniform to which he was accustomed.

"Nothing in hours," said the man, in response to a questioning flicker in the corner of the detective's eye. "A woman with a parasol this morning, a fat old gent and his spaniel, and a couple of tradesmen. It's not the Palace."

"It wouldn't be. Our game is no peacock. How soon until you're relieved?"

Clothing rustled. The lid of a watch popped open and snapped shut. "Two hours."

"Stretch your legs five minutes."

A gust of relief came from the doorway. "Thank you, sir. My back teeth are floating."

Morse nodded in parting and crossed the street, tossing the spent match onto the macadam.

The lobby was plain but for the desk, with laurels carved round the panels, an eastern rug of good workmanship, and a potted plant. Everything was spotless. The half-caste Chinese who greeted Morse from behind the desk wore a fresh collar and cuffs and his nails were scrubbed white. He combed his hair flat to his skull from a center part, with no trace of oil.

"Is Mr. Bolton in his room?"

Out of habit the clerk turned his head far enough to take in the keys hanging from pegs at his back. "No, sir. He left a few days ago to supervise his mining operations."

"When do you expect him back?"

"I cannot say for certain. He travels mainly on foot, so it would not be before the end of the week. Would you care to leave a message, Mr.——?"

"No, thank you. I'll be back later."

Outside, Morse cast aside his cigarette and walked away, shaking his head minutely for the benefit of the man who'd returned to his station opposite the hotel. Captain Stone was indeed a good man, but he expected all his officers to report to work with brass kidneys. Each was supplied with a sheet type-written by Jim Hume's secretary, with a detailed description of the man known to Thomas Ware as Charles E. Bolton:

Physical: square-shouldered, erect bearing, approx. 5'8", mid-fifties, white hair, imperial beard, moustache, blue eyes. Dress: suit, waistcoat, Chesterfield topcoat, bowler hat, stick.

"Not exactly guerrilla material," Hume had said after the pair had left Ware, with a stern warning not to attempt to make contact with his friend. "I wonder if we're not barking up the wrong tree."

"It wouldn't be the first time," Morse had replied.

If the chief were indeed entertaining second thoughts, his right-hand man was not.

*He travels mainly on foot*; not that he needed the confirmation, but it pleased him to know his instincts remained intact. He'd learned years ago to respect them, and they were telling him loud and clear that Bolton was their man.

He couldn't describe it in such a way that would sway a judge or a jury. It was a kind of buzz.

# TWENTY-ONE

*No man has lived till the Reaper he's met;*
*and come away with the best of the bet.*
*So 'twas with Black Bart, from the Angel of Night;*
*and with a fat bounty to show for his fright.*

I t had not gone well. He should have trusted his intuition.

The hammer dropped not during the chanciest moments, when intimidating the driver and maintaining that level of obedience were paramount, but in the first rush of success.

There had been no passengers this time, glory be to God. One could anticipate the reaction by Company employees, trained as they were in the situation; a civilian, on the other hand, might panic, swoon, or take it upon himself to perform an act he thought heroic. There had been that idiot woman who'd distracted him by flinging out her purse, and in one instance an armed passenger who thought his pocket pistol was there for a purpose, only to be dissuaded by a fellow traveler, who'd seized his arm and called him a damn fool, did he want to get us all killed? Better vacant seats, and that much of the human element subtracted.

However, an empty coach provided the Company with the opportunity to bolt the damn iron box inside rather than in the rear boot. Putting aside his native courtesy, Bolton had manhandled the driver by his upper arm into the rear-facing seat, out of reach of the shotgun laid on the one opposite while Bolton set to work with his hammer and bar. He'd gotten it open, distributed a poke of unrefined dust and a clanking pouch of coins among his overall pockets, retrieved the shotgun, and taken a step out into the open, when a blurred movement in the tail of his eye took the shape of a man with a long gun raised to his shoulder.

He never knew who the man was, and came to the conclusion later that it was a Company messenger who'd alighted from the coach as it approached the top of the hill—Bolton's own eight-year-old assault still fresh in memory—and taken cover with ambush in mind.

In the moment, no such reasoning was possible, or necessary. Black Bart bounded to the earth and ran.

At such times, the clock stood still. An eternity elapsed before something whined past his ear, followed close on by the bark of a report. He dove for the nearest thicket, unmindful of thorns. A flat, slapping noise might have been a slug nicking bark. Then he felt a sting and a hot gush flooding the back of his right hand. Running yet, branches thwacking his face and gouging at his eyes, he glanced down and saw blood dripping off the ends of his fingers.

He picked up his pace, flinging blood like lather from a racing horse, his breath sawing in his throat and his heart thudding between his ears, for what seemed miles before a wall of exhaustion smacked him head to toe. The flour sack collapsed and bellied, soaked through with his stale breath, suffocating him. For the second time in his career he snatched it off and cast it away. With it went his bowler. He hunched with his hands on his thighs, gasping and staining the right knee of his overalls with his own life-force. Shaking, he raised that hand and examined the purple furrow across the back, still pumping. He shook loose his handkerchief and bound it tight, setting the knot with his teeth. Immediately it stained through.

He ran again, head cocked for the sound of pursuit, until lungs and legs would have no more of it. The shotgun had grown as heavy as an anvil. He stumbled and almost fell over a fallen log, split open with rot and alive with grubs. Falling to his knees, he clawed at the pulpy wood with both hands—one throbbing—and jammed the shotgun muzzles-first into the crawling mass, covering it the rest of the way with sodden sawdust.

The wound, he discovered, when while walking he braved himself to unwind the makeshift bandage, was superficial; nothing like as alarming as the scar he still carried on his temple. He stuffed the sopping handkerchief into a pocket ("Would that I'd done the same the first time," he would tell reporters, when it was clear his race was run), and continued on his way at something like the pace of his leisurely strolls from San Francisco to gold country—a thousand years ago, it seemed to him then.

Through the day he walked, and when night came like a girder dropped from a building under construction, he spotted a log hut, dark and overgrown with lichens, the primordial sign of long desertion. There he spent the night, on a mattress gathered of moldy burlap sacks, with only his clasp knife to defend himself clutched in his good hand. When dawn woke him, he searched the cabin for a better weapon— and more urgently, for a tin of food or a pail of water—but found nothing more useful than a soft felt hat, but useful nonetheless, to replace his lost bowler. The leather sweatband was stained, but he could wear it without fear of being seen and remembered as a stranger wandering open country with nothing to protect his head from the elements.

One learned to be grateful for the little things; especially when he was still in possession of his hide and what turned out to be five hundred fifty dollars in gold coin and a poke of untraceable glittering dust. It was more than he'd ever taken away from a single robbery; and, by God, he'd earned it. When he came upon a stream he drank from it until he almost foundered.

The lights of Sacramento sparkled like shattered glass at the base of the last hill he would climb. He washed up in a bath house, changing a double eagle. The female clerk who took it frowned at the garish slash on his hand. She was a tall matron in a chignon, whalebone, and pleated linen; the very picture of a character in a drawing-room farce. "That looks nasty, sir. You'll want to have it looked at."

"I will indeed. Thank you." But it had scabbed over, and the flesh round it was a healthy pink. He'd soaped it gingerly and patted it dry with a fluffy white towel. Against all odds, the patron saint of pirates had defended it from infection.

His first stop was in a restaurant, not too genteel for a man in rough work clothes, where he helped himself to two servings of fried chicken, mashed potatoes, green vegetables in season, strawberry shortcake, and a pitcher of water. In a barbershop agleam with white porcelain and equipped with the latest eastern periodicals, the proprietor, a jolly Italian with ruddy cheeks and an impressive brace of handlebars, reacted not at all to his customer's dishevelment—in gold country, millionaires came in all packages—but beamed brighter at the flash of yellow. He swathed the man's face in a steaming towel (it put Bolton in mind, with a little sting of fresh fear, of his flour-sack hood), scraped away stubble, trimmed his hair and whiskers, and anointed him with bay rum. Feeling reborn, the patron told him to keep the change. He rarely tipped handsomely; but life was sweeter than ever, and why not share his good fortune? A man who had brushed so near the Great Imponderable must lose his dread of appearing conspicuous. He was flushed with a sense of immortality.

"You look a new man, signor." The barber brushed him off with gusto.

"Hardly that; but it is an improvement. Is there a good tailor in the neighborhood?"

The Italian enthusiastically endorsed one of the dearer establishments within walking distance. It was at the top of a flight of stairs open to the street with the shop's services painted on the risers. The tailor, dour and basset-faced—the opposite of the cheerful barber—fitted him with good worsted, two dress shirts, a collar, a green silk cravat, and a pearl-gray bowler; he stocked no footwear, but sent Bolton's boots out to be cleaned and polished, and as business was slow agreed to cut the suit while he waited; in return for an emolument, of course.

He mounted a velvet-covered stand and inspected the

results in a tri-fold mirror framed with cherubim. A businessman in tasteful dress looked back at him, the curled brim of his hat set square across his brow. The boy who'd blacked his boots had managed to dissemble the cuts Bolton had made in the toes to accommodate his corns.

*A new man indeed,* he thought; *or at least only slightly shopworn.*

"Shall I bundle your other things so you can take them with you?"

He turned to consider the garments he'd worn, clay-stained and dusty in a sorry heap on a chair. "Dispose of them. I shan't have need for them again."

Feeling more than respectable, he strolled down to the train station, where he braved a Pullman ticket to Reno, Nevada, just across the state border, for once dozing most of the way, and spent two days and nights in one of the better hotels. No one there knew him, as Boles or Bolton, and the gold roads were far enough away for stories of Black Bart to serve only as a diversion. The city had diversions of its own in plenty, with strangers arriving and departing by the carload. Questions as to the background of yet another visitor were not asked. He had no need to keep up the pretense of mining speculation, with such pitfalls of professional argot and details of the trade to watch out for.

It was a friendly place, then; especially for a man who enjoyed taking a plunge on the occasional game of chance. Gambling was rampant, despite state law; some years before, when a proposition appeared on the ballot to consider ejecting tinhorns from the city, all the betting places in town shut down for days; the eerie calm (and dead halt to business both legitimate and otherwise) led to a landslide defeat of the measure. Bolton wagered modestly on Faro in a well-appointed parlor called the Louvre, and came out ahead. More importantly, he exchanged the chips he'd bought for banknotes, which were less showy than gold coins. He splurged on a late squab supper in the restaurant upstairs, all snow-white linen and sterling silver, with a Grecian wraith plucking a harp.

The next morning, after dining on kippers and black coffee in his room, he went to the telegraph office and sent two wires: one to the owner of the Webb House, asking his room to be made ready for his return, the second to Thomas Ware in Bush Street, asking him to hold his laundry until he came to call for it.

# TWENTY-TWO

*Now, West isn't East, a poet once said;*
*and oceans apart must make up their bed.*
*But as night touches day, and present meets past,*
*Jim Hume and Black Bart faced each other at last.*

I'll have somebody's head for this. I'll grind his bones to make my bread!"

"Colorfully fabulistic," Hume said. "But perhaps it won't be necessary."

"Necessary?" John J. Valentine slapped his palm on his bare desk with a smack so loud his chief of detectives felt the sting. "By God, I'll bring an embargo against any more shipments from that country if the agents don't start posting shotgun messengers! Has it escaped you that this time the devil made off with more swag than from any of the past twenty-seven? Twenty-seven!" He flashed the number with spread fingers, opening and closing his hands three times. "And don't crank that hurdy-gurdy again about him showing the white feather after seeing the color of his blood! That's what Ben Thorn said the first time someone got the drop on him, and here he is again. While we're on that subject, when was the last time these fellows took target practice? Flesh wounds on both occasions, at a distance of yards! My grandson could have brought him down at that range with a pocket catapult."

"I can get him closer than that."

Whereupon James B. Hume put the general superintendent's mind at rest regarding his detective's almost supernatural calm.

It required diplomacy, as Valentine must never question why two men in his employ should take it upon themselves to keep him in the dark. He would be in danger of letting something slip to the journalists who hounded him every time Black Bart struck; and considering the man's present choleric state, Hume was content that he and Morse had made a wise decision.

The man in charge of the line wasn't the half of it, came to that. Somewhere in the long loose chain of communication between headquarters, station agents, and peace officers working the case, everything Hume hoped to keep out of the grasping hands of the press had spilled forth like spring runoff. One man could keep a secret; two, if one of them were Harry Morse. Captain Appleton Stone of the San Francisco Police was an unavoidable risk; his cooperation was vital, and he was at least a veteran who knew the rules. Thomas Ware, the tobacconist and Bolton's launderer, had had to be let in on the secret before he learned on his own why the men were so interested in his mining friend. (The newspapers might at any time drag Hume back onto the front page.) A party who thought he'd been played for a fool was twice as likely to tip off the target. Ware was under constant watch by Stone's officers, themselves ignorant of the identity of the man whose description they had committed to memory. Running to the boss before the trap was sprung could turn out to be a blunder as bad as what the Pinkertons had done in Clay County. Still, there was the danger of offending him, as if he were a man with little discretion. Which he was.

To Valentine's credit, however, he did not attempt to pump Hume for details. After a brooding circuit about the office, hands locked behind his back in a stranglehold, he nodded at the wisdom of silence. Hume formed a new respect for the man who'd hired him. Anyone who could surprise him after spending all these years with only a thin partition separating them was someone who deserved his loyalty.

"Henceforth I shall pay more heed to laundry marks and such truck," he said. "I congratulate you, Jim."

"It was luck; but that can be a skill. Harry did the hard work, and played Ware like a prize fish."

"Our fish still swims, remember. We must approach this one on tiptoe. No law prohibits a man from strolling the road or losing his handkerchief. Even if those witnesses who have met a man very like Bolton come forward, all we have is a traveler who put in for a night's lodging and a man sitting on a rock writing."

"Similarly, no law prohibits one man from drawing another into conversation."

"And if he slams the door in your face?"

"In the place I have in mind, there will be no door between us." Permitting himself one of his scarce smiles,

Hume drew forth a Western Union flimsy, wired from Reno, Nevada, to Thomas Ware at the Bush Street branch of the California laundry.

*　*　*

A dense November fog ringed the city like a moat at dawn. Streets, bridges, residences, and buildings of commerce were submerged, leaving only stone steeples and the Maypole arrangement of cable cars atop Telegraph Hill. They gave the impression of floating or, less substantially, shimmering; things that vanished at a blink.

Alighting from the train, he bought a copy of the *Herald* from a stand and read of Black Bart's latest assault on W. F. & Co. The party of officers and volunteers had recovered yet another flour-sack mask and this time a black bowler, and reported finding spots of blood in the path the robber had broken through foliage, confirming a report that he'd been wounded by gunfire, possibly fatally; but the journalist's account cast doubts on the evidence that the man himself had made his escape and that there were no signs of severe bleeding.

He loitered over the columns until he was alone on the platform, then peeled the sticking-plaster he'd applied to the back of his right hand to forestall infection. The burnt-orange scab was less conspicuous against tanned skin than the white gauze he dropped in an ash can.

The morning man was behind the desk of the Webb House. He handed Bolton his key with a smile. "You're looking particularly well turned-out today, sir. New clothes?"

"A reward for a wise investment. The books were especially healthy this trip."

"Do you need help with your valise?"

"Please send it up. I have an errand to run." He lifted it onto the desk.

Outside, the fog was lifting, curling now around the tops of trees with the mellow-gold autumn sun sliding underneath. It warmed the air, and he whistled "The Wells, Fargo Line" as he strolled, swinging a new stick. The notes he'd exchanged the coins for in the Louvre clung to his ribs with the warmth of a mustard plaster.

"Mr. Bolton! How was Reno?"

Mrs. Yee was not present. Thomas Ware had stepped in from his tobacco shop to manage the laundry. He sounded less than his amiable self; perhaps the old Chinese woman had left him to a busy morning.

"Rowdy, I'm afraid." The customer raised his brows at a man standing on his side of the counter, facing the newcomer rather than the proprietor: An Irishman from the look of him, but no Corktown ruffian. He wore a suit of clothes with a quiet check and an amiable expression.

"A man who wishes to meet you," Ware said. He made the introductions, adding: "Er, Mr. Hamilton is also in mining."

Although he'd formed a picture of his man based on his description, Harry Morse thought him an unlikely villain in the flesh. Broader across the shoulders than expected, straight-backed, and immaculately dressed in a gray suit cut to his measure with a double-breasted waistcoat, green cravat, and a pale gray bowler. His heavy moustache and chin-whiskers, both shot with gray, were neatly trimmed and he gripped an ebony stick by its gold knob, but not in a defensive gesture. The ferrule rested on the floor and there was no telltale bulge in the side pocket in which his other hand

rested. He could be taken for a high-ranking military officer retired before his usefulness was spent. His boots, although well-polished, were slashed round the toes; a fact
that set all Morse's cells vibrating.

Did those clear blue eyes sharpen at the prospect of meeting a man who knew more about the science of mining
than the average? Difficult to tell. The former sheriff and
longtime detective was adept at reading suspicion on the
faces of men who themselves warranted suspicion; but in
these mild features, the cheekbones high and the brow
prominent, he saw nothing more than curiosity in the presence of an interested stranger.

And by God, if Morse hadn't worked as closely with Jim
Hume as he had for seven years, no creature on earth would
have found fault with him for mistaking the two.

Bolton, for his part, allowed himself a small smile, and it
was genuine. Although he avoided intimacy with so-called
colleagues in the trade, he knew enough about it from physical experience and applied study to pass himself off on casual acquaintance. The successful miners he'd known rarely
talked shop, preferring to blend in with the civilized peoples
of San Francisco society rather than discuss the earthy ori-
gins of their fortunes; a word about hydraulics, a phrase of
working jargon dropped into a bit of conversation about
something else, and then the discourse moved on to safer
subjects: horse racing, the fights, the opera season. He took
his hand from his pocket and gave the man as good a grip
as he got; and if Mr. Hamilton's glance flicked toward his
scratch; well, hadn't his new acquaintance just returned from
a tour of his operations in the Mother Lode?

"I wonder, Mr. Bolton, if you could spare a few moments? I have a business proposition that I think will prove beneficial for us both."

Did a muscle twitch in a bronzed cheek? Morse could be sure of nothing about Bolton. He tightened his grasp. The other appeared not to notice this, and hesitated only briefly before nodding. "If Mr. Ware will oblige me by keeping my goods a few moments more."

Ware could; and if air gushed from his lungs when the pair turned toward the street door, it might have been the weary sigh of a man resigned to resuming his work.

Pedestrian traffic was picking up. It became a busy crowd when they turned from Bush onto Montgomery, but the two men's business dress and steady stride opened a path that led all the way to the front door of the headquarters of Wells, Fargo, & Co.

Furtively (he hoped), Morse pressed closer to his companion as they neared the building. If his man bolted, taking to the cover of the crowd the same way he slid between trees from the site of a robbery, he wasn't likely to resurface. Black Bart did not belong to the simpleton race that normally ran to his profession.

But Bolton kept his easy pace as they entered the lobby. "Have you an office here?"

"I'm borrowing one from a friend. I hope you're not one of those people who distrust banks."

"Not at all. I sometimes do business here."

The revelations kept piling up, each more astounding than the one before.

They went through a door and up a steep flight of steps. The air was thick with the smell of stale cigars. The odor, and the smoke that created it, grew tangible as they entered a glass-paneled door that stood open to the hallway at the top of the landing. A young man sat at a small writing table facing a desk heaped high with shabby leather portfolios. Another man, close to Bolton's age, build, and general appearance rose from behind it.

"Mr. Charles Bolton," said the polite Mr. Hamilton—and for the first time his voice wobbled a little—"Mr. James Hume."

# TWENTY-THREE

*Two cocks in a circle will dance a ballet,*
*an old bull and a young one will square off to slay.*
*The contest's as ancient as Heaven and Hell,*
*with challenged and challenger 'waiting the bell.*

The two middle-aged men shook hands, their opposing profiles matching so closely they might have shared the same blood. Morse took Bolton's hat and hung it on the halltree next to Hume's unprepossessing slouch. The guest preferred to keep his stick, and sat when Hume did, facing the desk with his feet flat on the floor and his hands folded on the knob. Morse closed the door, scraped round a spare chair, and seated himself. From here on in he was content with the role of spectator, with the omnipresent Thacker taking notes.

He and the chief had discussed this. Some men subjected to questioning crumbled in the crossfire, others sealed themselves shut the moment they felt themselves outnumbered by the enemy. In the same instant, both detectives had seen in which category Charles E. Bolton belonged.

Hume began by unstopping a fat jar containing a dozen

202 ★ LOREN D. ESTLEMAN

bullet-shaped cigars standing on their blunt ends and tilting it toward his guest, who raised a polite palm and shook his head. The chief's brows lifted questioningly; the palm turned over in a conciliating gesture, and Hume selected a cigar, bit off the end, spat it into his waste basket, and set fire to it with a square wooden match, blowing gales of smoke toward the ever-widening gyre on the ceiling. For full a minute and a half after the men had sat down, not a word had passed between them.

"Have we met, Mr. Bolton?" Hume opened. "I have a talent for remembering faces."

"I think it likely, Mr. Hume. As I told Mr. Hamilton, I sometimes have business downstairs."

"Indeed. Do you conduct all your business here?"

"No. The Panic taught me not to place all my eggs in a single basket."

"A sound policy. I recognized you at once as a cautious man."

Bolton's eyes glinted. "As are most men, once they get to be our age."

"Perhaps the Company has had the privilege of transporting some of the profits from your mine; or is it *mines*? Mr. Ware wasn't specific, according to Hamilton."

"We've never discussed my activities in detail. I maintain a full interest in several operations, and a partnership in a number of others." He unfolded his hands from his stick and refolded them the other way. "I'd not be surprised that my managers have made use of your services, although I could not say for certain. I'm no longer involved with the day-to-day operation. I trust such details to the good office of the men I've placed in charge."

That phrase, "the good office," echoed in Morse's ears. *In that respect, I honor only the good office of Wells, Fargo.* The special agent had committed all of Black Bart's reported remarks to memory. This was the first fissure in the marble façade; not that anything in his appearance indicated he was aware of having stepped wrong. Hume's own countenance remained seamless.

"I can provide that certainty, if you'll tell me where the mines are located."

"They're in the Lode country. I confess to ignorance as to the specific counties. It's been many years since I filed."

"Did you come out here in forty-nine?"

"Fifty."

"The same year as I, although things didn't break for me the way they did for you. I broke even the first year, then went even broker the second." Hume smiled apologetically at this weak attempt at wit. "The Lucky Lucy, that was what I called my claim. I can see now that was begging the issue—or rather the lack of it. How do you call yours?"

"I never assigned them names, only numbers."

"I wish I'd thought of that. It's best not to place much sentimentality in something that may not return the affection."

"So I've found. I've sunk an empty shaft or two in my time."

"You filed under the name Bolton?"

"I did not."

This response, as final as it was calm, bore out what Morse had learned from Ware. He would hate to sit across a poker table from Bolton.

Hume, of course, would relish it.

Once again, the visitor rearranged his hands on the stick.

204 ★ LOREN D. ESTLEMAN

Was this a sign of restlessness at last? "Mr. Hamilton mentioned something about a proposition."

"Yes, we'll get to that. I prefer to know a bit about a fellow and his holdings before I propose doing business with him. If you can give me those numbers and the name you filed under, I'll look them up in Sacramento. Mr. Thacker?"

The secretary turned to a fresh page in his writing-block and dipped a pen.

"We're much alike," Bolton said. "You've seen me, you surmise; but I know your face definitely, from the newspapers. You're Wells, Fargo's chief of detectives, are you not? What business can you have with a mining speculator?"

"I'm nearing the age of retirement. I don't intend to die at this desk. I've put aside some money and am looking for a place to invest it. I assume you need to replace your equipment from time to time, hire good men, who don't come cheap. The fresh funds will be useful, and I would request only a modest percentage of the proceeds. I should like to visit your mines in the Mother Lode."

"Did I say the Mother Lode? I beg your pardon. My properties are all on the east face of the Sierra, near the Nevada line. I am just back from visiting them, with a brief stop to rest in Reno afterward."

Hume frowned at the end of his cigar. "It's I who must ask your forgiveness. I was under the impression you were in gold, not silver."

His hands traded places a third time.

"I'm sorry if I expressed myself in such a way that you would place that construction on what I said. In San Francisco, when people learn you're in mining, they make certain assumptions that one doesn't trouble to correct."

"I see." Although it was clear from Hume's manner that he did not. "We do a fair amount of business on that side of the Sierra. I should like to inspect one of your properties, if you can give me its location."

Blue eyes searched the floor, as if a map were engraved on it. "Directions in this case are difficult. I generally approach them from memory."

"If you're at liberty any time soon, perhaps you'll be kind enough to perform as my guide."

"Having just returned from there, I don't expect to be at liberty for at least a month. I have transactions awaiting attention in the city." He lifted his gaze. "You're trespassing upon my convenience. May I inquire as to the real reason for invading my privacy?"

"You came at my associate's invitation. No one compelled you to accept it."

"I was lured here on the promise of a proposition."

"So it is, and we shall come to it. May I in turn inquire as to your evasive answers to my questions?"

"If they are evasive, it's because the questions are impertinent. Gentlemen do not engage in badgery, nor do they submit to it."

A fine thread of steel ran through his tone. Morse fought the temptation to lean forward in his chair. The crack had begun to open. He could not risk sealing it with an eager movement.

"We are nearly done." Which was a lie the chief took no trouble to make convincing. "My mission is quite important, as will presently be made plain. You must agree it's every citizen's duty to cooperate with authorities in the interest of justice."

"That, sir, would depend upon your definition of the term."

"Authority? It's true I'm not a sworn officer of the law, but I enjoy the cooperation of—"

"Not authority. Justice."

Hume, the master commander of the Company's department of war, switched to a frontal assault.

"How did you come to injure your hand?"

Bolton frowned at the scar. "I caught it on the vestibule alighting from the train in Truckee."

"Have you a mine near there?"

"No. I got off to stretch my legs on the way to Reno."

"Near Reno, then."

"This is becoming intolerable." Bolton began to lever himself to his feet. Now both detectives leaned forward, resembling predatory birds. He resettled himself.

"Will you allow us to accompany you to your room at the Webb House?" Hume asked. "I'm certain this can all be cleared up there."

"Certainly not. You've squandered enough of my time as it is."

At a signal from the chief, Morse rose, slid open the top drawer of the nearest filing case, and deposited the object he'd removed from it atop the accumulation on the desk. With the elaborate care of a haberdasher, Hume lifted the black bowler by its brim in both hands and offered it to Bolton. "Would you indulge me by trying this on?"

The man seated opposite him said nothing, leaving his hands folded on his stick.

"Mr. Morse?"

If Bolton noted the sudden disappearance of a "Mr. Hamilton" from his orbit, he showed no trace.

The special agent and his superior had blocked out every movement in this performance. Still standing, he lifted the pearl-gray bowler he'd placed on the halltree and examined the tag stitched to the leather sweatband. "Seven and an eighth."

Hume turned over the hat he held and examined the tag; another bit of theater mounted for the benefit of their guest. If anyone knew Black Bart's hat size as well as Black Bart himself, it was he. He looked from it to Bolton, who smiled thinly.

"It's a common measurement. Is it your intention to question every man in town who wears seven and an eighth?"

"I may go to that trouble. But before we disturb half the local male population, tell me what is your opinion of this?"

No file drawer this time, but Hume's own pocket produced a square of linen, once white but now stained copiously, not the least from much handling. He took it by the top corners, held it up, and let it unfurl like a sail.

To his man's credit, he wasted none of their time arguing the handkerchief's ownership; the laundry mark was quite visible, and he seemed to be aware of the establishment's policy of individualizing each item.

"I confess I didn't miss it. I purchase them in sets of five. May I ask where it was found?"

"May I ask where it was lost?"

"Again, I cannot say. If I kept track of such things I suppose I wouldn't be so absentminded as to have misplaced it."

"It was found near the scene of the attempted robbery of one of our shipments near the town of Strawberry."

"I don't know the place. I suppose whoever came upon my handkerchief claimed it for his own. I would not expect a highwayman to scruple about returning it. That he should lose it himself strikes me as ironic."

"I submit that you lost it fleeing for your life, after a round from an express manager's shotgun cut that crease across your temple. You're a fortunate man, Mr. Black Bart. Bullets seem to bounce off you like sleet."

His guest blinked. "My name is Bolton."

# TWENTY-FOUR

*A man whose feet may leave no trace,*
*still lays down a trail that leads to his face.*
*For when you make your living from theft,*
*you can yet be track'd by the hole that you left.*

The interview came to an end after three hours. It was nearly midnight. The man who called himself Bolton was visibly exhausted, his collar wilting and his face haggard, as if the skull had shrunken away from the skin. He offered no objection when officers came in response to a message sent by courier to take him to the city jail; he appeared relieved that the ordeal was over, if only for a while.

Morse, who had done little more than listen for discrepancies Thacker might overlook in Bolton's answers, felt nearly as played out. Hume alone appeared as fresh as at the beginning. The chief seemed to draw energy from approaching victory.

The suspect's day was over, but his captors had hours to go before they slept. At the Webb House, a wide-eyed clerk conducted them, accompanied by Captain Stone with a warrant, to Bolton's room.

With Morse recording the inventory in a notebook, Hume opened a travel-worn valise and laid out its contents on the bed: A hatchet, its wooden haft rubbed to a high gloss from handling; a pinch bar, blunted at the cleft end; and changes of shirts, stockings, and underthings, still creased from the haberdasher's shelves. It contained no shotgun, nor was one found in the wardrobe or under the mattress, which Hume rent all round with a clasp knife and probed the horsehair stuffing for hidden items.

Two sets of overalls—spares, no doubt—were folded neatly on the floor of the wardrobe. They matched Black Bart's attire as described by witnesses; but so did thousands of pairs sold in San Francisco.

The drawer in the nightstand reaped a harvest of large- and small-scale maps of the Mother Lode country, stagecoach schedules for the region, and a page of foolscap partially covered with script written in a neat, clerkly hand; a letter, the content suggested, the intended recipient unknown. Hume and Morse, who had stored all of the loops and tails of Black Bart's handwritten poetry in their memories, agreed that there were many similarities.

Stone said, "I've never testified in a trial in which a man's handwriting swayed the jury either way. We can't convict a man for writing a letter, owning dungarees and some tools, and blowing his nose in good linen."

Hume returned his attention to the drawer. Inside lay a Bible bound in pebbled black cloth, of the kind frequently provided by places of lodging. He laid it atop the nightstand, pulled the drawer all the way out, examined the bottom and back, and peered into the space it left. No incriminating evidence was fixed to the woodwork. A methodical man, he put the drawer back on its slides and picked up the Bible to return it. He hesitated, then lifted the cover. A yellowed slip of paper adhered from years of contact to the front flyleaf, bearing a penciled legend in a hand different from Bolton's own:

> *This precious Bible is presented to Charles E. Boles, First Sergeant, Company B, 116th Volunteer Illinois Infantry, by his wife as a New Year's gift. May God bring him home in faith. Decatur, Illinois, 1 January 1865.*

"Boles," said Morse. "How many names can one fellow have?"

Hume stood in the center of the room, drumming his fingers on the book. Setting it down, he swung about, scooped up the empty valise, and rummaged through the interior, thrusting a hand deep into each of the pockets in the lining. He felt something balled up in a corner. It was stuck there, as if it had been jammed in hard. He closed his fist round coarse cloth and worried at it. When it came loose he pulled out a small sack. He opened it and reached inside.

He drew out a handful of something that glittered when it streamed between his fingers.

Stone, a tall, gaunt man who looked even more so in his snug uniform, both rows of brass buttons polished bright, was of an age similar to the detectives, but his burnsides and military-brush moustaches were as black as anthracite.

"By God," he said. "I told my boy Midas was just a story."

Hume hefted the sack on his palm, then passed it to Morse, who did the same. The police captain took it last.

"Six ounces, give or take." He returned it.

"Give." Hume jiggled the sack. "This and a month's pay says it's six and a quarter. That was the amount stolen from Funk Hill."

Morse said, "Where is his weapon?"

"Buried somewhere in gold country. He left in a hurry, and would want to lighten his load. We'll find it."

"Maybe in all that digging we'll make a fresh strike for ourselves before the century turns."

The chief scooped everything back into the valise and snapped the latches. "Why go to the bother, when we can just ask the man who buried it?"

\* \* \*

On a combined total of four hours' sleep, the Company men approached a windowless cell in the square brick box of the jail. The corridor was dark but for the circle of orange light shed by the turnkey's lantern. Like its neighbors, the cell was made of steel slats riveted together and the building constructed around it. The man sat upright on a cot chained to the wall with his feet on the floor and his hands resting on his thighs. The feet were clad in thick woolen stockings. His slashed boots stood at the foot of the cot, their tired shanks drooping.

He looked more rested than his visitors felt, and trim in

the white shirt and gray trousers he'd worn with his suit, minus collar and cravat, but with the top button fastened at his throat. His hair and whiskers were tidy, slicked down with water; a white enamel bucket was provided for drinking. His blue eyes were bright as a bird's.

Hume and Morse remained standing. The chief held out the Bible. "You might find comfort in it."

"Thank you." The man on the cot took it and laid it beside him without taking his eyes off Hume.

"Which is it?" Hume asked. "Bolton or Boles?"

"My name is Charles E. Bolton." No trace of belligerence showed in the man's tone.

"We're sorry to have to rouse you so early," Hume said, "but you can sleep on the boat. You'll need this; it's chilly out." From under one arm he produced a Chesterfield overcoat and tossed it onto the cot. "I got Ware to open early: You forgot to pick up your laundry. We're taking you by river to Stockton, and from there to Calaveras County."

Bolton lifted his wrists obligingly.

Hume shook his head. "You won't be in manacles. We'd rather not attract public attention. The journals are at present unaware that Black Bart is under arrest."

"He is not; but I give you my word I will not attempt to escape. My innocence will free me soon enough."

"A thief's word is written on sand. Captain Stone will accompany us. You will be among armed men who will not hesitate to shoot you down if you try anything."

Harry Morse thought the chief was being unnecessarily harsh now that the bird was in hand. It appeared that eight years of frustration and the jeering of the press had been building up like magma waiting to erupt.

It would get worse.

\* \* \*

A riverboat is no place for restful sleep. Unlike its oceangoing counterparts, theirs drew a shallow draft, and its passengers were aware of each shift and yaw as it navigated the swift current, like a swimming creature on whose back they rode. As the wedding-cake craft steamed westward, its paddle wheels churning the San Joaquin into a silver-white froth, the four men sat side by side on rigid wooden benches, over-coated and with their hats screwed down tight against chill air laced with tissues of fog. Their breath made jets of gray.

Hume, more sanguine now, made conversation. "Is this how you started your journeys, or did you walk the whole way?"

"I haven't been in this country for years."

"As you like. I'll be getting off in Clinton. I'm expected in the valley. It may surprise you to know Black Bart isn't the only business of interest to the Company."

"It neither surprises nor concerns. I am no business at all."

It certainly came as a surprise to Morse, who glanced at Stone and from his expression knew that he was not alone in this; but neither man commented.

The prisoner sat back, folding his hands across his spare middle and closing his eyes, but still he didn't sleep. He seemed to be humming to himself. Morse, seated be-side him, leaned closer, pressing a palm to his opposite ear against the throbbing bellow of foghorns, panting of the steam engine, and swosh-swosh-swosh of the paddles to listen: It was "The Wells, Fargo Line."

In Clinton, on the Alameda County side of the bay, Hume stood, and at a nod from him Morse rose and joined him at the rail. His superior lit a cigar, shielding the flame of the match from the wind. "Sheriff Thorn's awaiting a wire. Have him meet you in Stockton."

Morse was champing to ask what business could be so important as to take the chief away from the prize of his career; but he knew better than to question him about something he had not chosen voluntarily to confide.

They parted on the dock. Morse sent the message and re-boarded just as the boat resumed moving. He found the others where he'd left them, Stone looking greenish, but with the fierce expression he wore on all official occasions intact. Their captive was dozing. If the special agent had entertained any doubts as to the identity of the man they were escorting, they left him then. Here was all the outward serenity Bolton had carried into Hume's office, and into harm's way no fewer than twenty-eight times on the outlaw trail.

As the pitch of the engine changed, reversing the action of the paddles to slow its progress, the Stockton dock, whitewashed and hung with sandbags to keep the hull from colliding with the timbers, came out of fog; and with it a crowd of people that must surely have strained the deep-sunk supporting posts to the limit. Morse saw the familiar uniform of shapeless, unwashed overcoats and greasy bowlers peculiar to the journalist class, and on a makeshift platform built of packing cases, something that confirmed it: the black-painted wooden box of a tripod camera, a tray heaped with magnesium powder, and a stick of smoldering pitch held by the man crouched behind it; and the special agent was very glad that his chief wasn't present.

# TWENTY-FIVE

*Ev'ry legend has three acts, just like a Greek play;*
*in the first he's a phantom, no face to display;*
*when the next curtain rises, his image is known;*
*at the end of Act Three, he's Olympus's own.*

With a shared oath, Morse and Stone manhandled Bolton to his feet and inserted themselves in a scrum of debarking passengers, which formed a phalanx between them, the flock of journalists, and the photographer on his perch, all of whom scanned the crowd for a glimpse of James Hume, the only member of the expected party they could be certain to recognize by sight. Only then did the special agent grasp the reason for the chief's abrupt absence. Knowing the sly ways of scribblers, he'd held little faith in the arrangements he'd made to keep the thing under wraps, and by taking himself away had prevented them from drawing a straight line from the familiar predator to his faceless prey.

"I just wish the old man preferred bridge to poker," said Stone through clenched teeth. "It helps to inform your partners how you plan to bid."

Which remark told Morse the captain had reached the same conclusion as he.

They were approaching the end of the dock and the press of bodies relaxing round them—threatening to expose to scrutiny a party of three, with a man held fast in its center—when a hand gripped Morse's upper arm tight enough to bruise the muscle. "This way," came a harsh whisper. "The milk wagon."

Morse almost failed to recognize Ben Thorn without his sheriff's star. On the other side of the trio, a younger man built as stoutly had Stone's arm in a similar grasp. Before them, drawn alongside a berm separating the dock from a street paved with limestone, stood a wooden box mounted on bicycle wheels, hitched to a white mare wearing blinders. The legend GOLDEN STATE DAIRY was painted in bright copper circus letters on the side of the wagon. It was closed in all round and there was something suspiciously official-looking about the man in the driver's seat, despite the white overalls common to milk deliverymen.

Inside, there were no shining steel cans, no stacks of carrying racks filled with bottles of milk. Instead, the men from San Francisco found themselves seated on a bench facing Thorn, his deputy, and a man unknown to Morse, wearing a shirt without a collar under a rusty black suit redolent of moth powder and cedar.

"This is Martin," Thorn said.

Morse knew the name. Thomas P. Martin was the miner whose cabin Hume had put into on his way from the scene of the robbery near Strawberry; the man who at first had mistaken the chief for the drifter the Company had decided was Black Bart. His face, seamed beyond its apparent years and brown, brightened when his gaze fell upon Bolton; then grew grave. He looked at Thorn and nodded.

"This is the man who came to stay with you on the night of June fourteenth last?" The date had coincided with the robbery of the Wells, Fargo shipment driven by Thomas Forse near Little Lake.

"Yes, definitely."

Bolton said, "I've never seen this man before in my life." He turned his face toward the side of the wagon, as if there were a window there to look out.

Harry Morse felt a stab of disappointment. That the man who had laid siege to the Company for eight years, vanishing each time into thin air, should say anything so predictable took the shine off his and Hume's triumph. This was no mastermind; merely a clever felon with more than his fair share of luck.

"Thank you, Mr. Martin." Thorn reached back over his shoulder and rapped his knuckles against the front of the wagon. There was a flapping of lines and then the vehicle started forward, the horse's shaggy hoofs clip-clopping with a measured tread. "We'll put you off at your hotel. Please stay in your room until someone comes for you."

"How long will that be?" asked the prospector.

"That would depend upon the gentlemen of the press."

"Who alerted the journals?" Morse asked the sheriff after their witness had alighted.

"I shouldn't like to say. I thought it politic to notify the sheriff's offices in all the counties where Bart operated. Whom they told—" He rolled his shoulders. "These scalawags are capable of concealing a spy under some wife's petticoats."

Morse didn't believe him. The man was hanging on to his job by the ghost of his stale reputation, and this tardy show of covert action was theater, staged for the Company's benefit. He'd be the first to cry victory.

A mob of the scalawags awaited them in the sheriff's office attached to the San Joaquin County Jail, a fairly new building that looked as if it had been transported there from a place of drawbridges and dungeons. The brickwork was whitewashed and there were plain chairs, a table, and a pot-bellied stove. Morse, appointed spokesman, turned aside questions barked out of all order and guided them through cursory details, crediting Hume with the discovery of the handkerchief and repeating several times—lest any of the cooperating agencies feel slighted—the importance of the concerted effort involving all the local authorities and the police department of San Francisco.

"Get that thing away from me!"

Morse had been addressing the reporters with his back to the prisoner, flanked by Stone and San Joaquin County deputies. A man—it might have been the same photographer from the dock; they all looked alike crouched behind their contraptions—had stepped from the crowd of journalists and was unfolding his tripod. Ben Thorn, standing behind Bolton, caught Morse's eye and rolled his shoulders again; it was a signal of surrender.

"Don't be bashful," said the man setting up the camera. "Lady Astor would be proud to share a shot with a gent like you."

Morse allowed to himself that this wasn't far from the truth. The turnkeys in San Francisco had returned the rest of Bolton's suit of clothes, including the bowler, and with his fine overcoat hanging fashionably open, he would not appear out of place on Nob Hill, or for that matter New York's Fifth Avenue. Bolton appeared to consider this, turning to look at himself in a tin mirror hanging on a nail. He adjusted the angle of the hatbrim, shot his cuffs, tugged down the corners of his waistcoat, squinted at the result. Turning back, he observed the photographer filling his hod with combustible powder from a square tin.

"Will that thing go off? Because I should like to go off myself."

The journalists' chuckles drowned under the scratching of pencils.

The man with the camera grinned behind walrus moustaches. "Don't worry; I haven't lost a subject yet."

Humor served, the pair settled down to serious business.

Bolton sat motionless in one of the split-bottom chairs, started when the magnesium went up in a sheet of white flame followed by the rotten-egg stench of sulfur.

"Will you stand up for another?"

He complied. The photographer studied the erect figure, then pointed at the small diamond pin fixing the cravat to his shirtfront. "Is that part of the loot?"

"Young man, don't be impertinent."

The standing pose was the one most frequently circulated: The celebrity buccaneer in the finest tailoring, a hand resting in an overcoat pocket with the thumb outside, the stick held at his hip like a general's baton, and the well-worn boots cut to ease his famous corns, would become an icon, reproduced in newspapers (transcribed into newsprint-friendly pen-and-ink), books, and *cards de visite* sold in photographic studios and general stores across the North

American continent; and the legend of the Gentleman Bandit become indelible. Morse, watching Charles E. Bolton—Boles—*bonvivant* Charlie of Ocean View Park, the Grand Opera House, and the dining room of the Palace Hotel, but always and forever "Black Bart, the Po8"—striking the most flattering attitude, his face stern as John Pierpont Morgan's fresh from plundering Wall Street.

The special agent for Wells, Fargo, & Co. stifled a classic Irish grin. He was watching a monolith in the making.

# TWENTY-SIX

*This was the story of bandit Black Bart;*
*who used the gold country to practice his art.*
*His brush was a shotgun, his canvas the road,*
*as he painted his way 'cross the old Mother Lode.*

"Got anything stronger?"

Inmate No. 11046 looked over the tops of his spectacles at the young man dressed as he, in San Quentin's signature vertical stripes and gripping his pillbox cap. His face was sallow, the cheeks sunken where molars were missing.

"Sorry, son. Allen's is the best I can do." He slid the small brown bottle across the scarred counter. "It's the best lung balsam on the market and will clear out some of the infernal dust from the jute mill."

As if reminded, the young man coughed rackingly into his fist. When the spasm passed, he picked up the bottle and looked at the face on the label. "Who's the whiskers?"

"Mr. Allen, ostensibly; though he bears a certain resemblance to Dr. Sloan and St. Jacob, of the rheumatism oil. Read the directions. Make sure you understand them."

He moved his lips over the words. "C-colds, crowp—"

"Croup. It's a pulmonary ailment, like yours."

"As-asth-th-th—"

"Asthma." Eleven-oh-forty-six lowered his voice. "Son, have you your letters?"

Muscles stood out on either side of the young inmate's narrow jaw. "I can write my name, if that's what you're about."

"What brought you to this place?"

"The doc in the infirmary. He—"

"I mean San Quentin."

"They said I burned down a barn."

"Was anyone hurt?"

"Only the cheap sonofabitch the barn belonged to, right in the pocketbook." He began coughing again.

A slim volume bound in tatters made its way from a shelf under the counter into his hands.

He squinted at the cover. "Mug—" He blushed and fell silent, his jaw muscles flexing.

"McGuffey. It's a first reader. I smuggled it out of the library, just in case. The literacy level here is abysmal."

"Ab—"

The mild face broke into a nest of humorous wrinkles. "You'll learn its meaning. I used to teach school."

"I got no use for schoolteachers."

"I won't take a ruler to you. If I do my job well and you learn to read labels and prescriptions, I will talk to Warden Edgar. I need an assistant. Unless you prefer choking in sack alley?" This was the jute mill. Without waiting for an answer, he nodded at the book. "Make what you can of it and come back an hour before lights out."

In the yard, pacing in a circle of men wearing identical plumage, the young inmate spoke over his shoulder to the man behind him, in a murmur stamped out by marching feet before it could reach the ears of the guards on exercise duty. "You know the pill-pusher in the pharmacy?"

The man, twice the other's age, replied in a grumbling bass. "Everybody knows Charlie. What about him?"

"What'd he do, run off with the school cash box and a girl from the fifth grade?"

"Armed robbery."

"The hell you say!"

"Shut up, you!"

The other made no reply until they'd circled far of the guard who'd shouted, pointing his truncheon. "Stagecoaches."

"Holy Christ." The young convict spoke in a tone even lower than at the start. "More than one?"

"Right around fifty, I reckon, all belonging to Wells, Fargo, and all by himself."

Another circuit in awed silence.

"He's in for a hundred years, I bet."

"Just six. He swore he never loaded his shotgun and they believed him."

"Wisht I got his jury."

"They were inclined his direction. He gave up the whole story—as much of it as they could prove already—and told them where they could find what he stole." His grumble turned to gurgling amusement. "He had it deposited with Wells, Fargo, under a trick name the whole time."

"What's his right name?"

"Boles, though he prefers Bolton. Can't say why."

"How come I never heard of him?"

"Sure you did."

Working in the pharmacy, busying himself with reorganizing the inventory—his predecessor, paroled a month before his appointment, had employed a system, if system it was, entirely his own, mysterious to all others—serving efficiently as an orderly in the prison infirmary, and helping fellow inmates to escape the murderous conditions in the jute mill and machine shop, Bolton managed to forget himself. Alone in his cell, attempting to work up interest rereading a classic he'd checked out of the library, he found himself dwelling upon past transgressions.

Not his robberies; they'd been an ongoing campaign against the ruthless faceless Company that he was convinced had contributed to Davy's death, and thus were a comfort he took to innocent sleep. It amused him further to follow the *Examiner*'s attacks upon James B. Hume for allowing the rival *Call* and the "boondock papers" he'd allowed to scoop them when Black Bart was brought at last to justice; typically, William Randolph Hearst's organ had preferred to blame someone in authority rather than its own failure to send a correspondent to the San Joaquin Jail. Such petty injustices were small enough redress for the massive injustice wrought by Wells, Fargo. Just now the editors were pillorying Hume for the light sentence he'd received. Of the nearly threescore assaults he'd made on the gold shipments, a jury of his peers had found him guilty only of the last robbery at Funk Hill. Charged the journal:

> What is the result of this perversion of justice? A few
> detectives divide a few thousand [unreported] dollars
> and instill in the dime-novel-charged heads of ten

thousand youths of this city the idea that one has to
be but a bold and successful robber to force the united
detective talent of the coast to intercede with judges
and obtain light sentences and get two-column no-
tices in the papers.

The columnist conjectured that four thousand dollars of
Black Bart's booty had been "hidden in the woods near
Copperopolis" and had found its way into the pockets of
Company employees.

Would that that were true; if in fact the sum total of his
takings had amounted to so much. If still concealed, it
would represent a comfort in his declining years. He had,
in fact, spent it all, and quite wisely: on horses, fighters, the
opera, fine meals, and the occasional woman.

In the end, it had been those six-and-a-quarter ounces of
unrefined dust that turned the tide; although the story of
the discarded handkerchief had become so entrenched in
his legend it would likely outlive all the principals.

The regrets he saved may have been for Elizabeth and
her daughters, the family he'd forsaken. His wife wrote,
amazingly enough, from Missouri, having learned of Black
Bart's true identity in the wire columns, offering forgiveness
and a return to the fold upon his release; but he could not
find in him the courage to respond in kind. He wrote back
in phrases too stiff for the standards of a celebrated poet, professing no love. Whether he was as callous as his language, or
desired to spare those he'd left behind further pain, cannot
be determined. Certainly something had died during that
bleak return to the deserted house in New Oregon, Iowa.

James B. Hume thought the worst of him for his flight

from responsibility, and expressed only contempt for this behavior in response to journalistic romancing of the poetic bandit who forbore violence.

Bolton found comfort in writing witty "apologies" to some of the stagecoach drivers he'd victimized, and even the shotgun messengers who'd managed to draw blood from the elusive Black Bart. He signed off:

> I am yours, dear sir, in haste.
>
> B.B.
>
> P.S. But not in quite so much a hurry as on the former occasion.

In recognition of exemplary behavior and aid in the interest of the "reform" of some of his fellow inmates (for so the prison board interpreted the purpose of his tutoring), Prisoner No. 11046, recorded in the files of San Quentin under the name Charles E. Boles, was paroled on January 21, 1888, having served four years and two months of a six-year sentence.

A gaggle of journalists stood on the wharf outside the prison, stamping their feet and blowing thick vapor into the cold wind coming off the slaty surface of the bay, when an upright figure came into view. They sprang to attention, as if in the presence of a foreign dignitary. The man was not as elderly as anticipated, wearing the suit, overcoat, and style of bowler fashionable five years before; but wearing them as if he'd just stepped from the pages of this quarter's *Gentleman's Own*. Clearly he had no need of the support of his gold-headed stick, which he raised—not threateningly, but in the manner of an orchestra conductor lifting his baton, to staunch the flow of queries.

"Your pardon, gentlemen. I'm a bit deaf these days and can listen to but one question at a time."

"How was prison, Mr. Boles?"

"Bolton. I should not care to repeat the experience. In addition to losing my hearing and my ability to read without spectacles, I forfeited more than four years of my life; which at fifty-five is no small sacrifice."

"What are your plans now?"

"They're indistinct. At one time I considered applying for a druggist's license; but things look different inside."

"What about taking up your old trade?"

He looked at the man who'd asked the question, staring at him over the top of his writing-block. He'd identified himself as an employee of the *San Francisco Chronicle*. "If it's mining you mean, I'm too old to swing a pick. If it's teaching school, I doubt any would have me."

"I mean robbing stagecoaches."

"The question is insolent. I am through with the business of crime."

"Will you return to your family?" asked another.

A whistle blasted.

"Gentlemen, my boat approaches."

"Perhaps you'll write poetry."

He'd turned toward the vessel crossing the bay. He swung back on the man from the *Chronicle*. "Young man, didn't you just hear me say I would commit no more crimes?"

\* \* \*

San Francisco looked bigger than he remembered. After an eight-by-eight cell and the narrow passages of the brick

230 LOREN D. ESTLEMAN

rectangle of San Quentin, even its side streets seemed as wide as boulevards, and his simply furnished room in the Nevada, a boardinghouse on Sixth Street, a suite at the Palace Hotel. He was not lonely; Mrs. Burling was an attentive landlady of some culture, who enjoyed discussing literature, music, and the theater with her new lodger, and there was always someone loitering in a doorway across the street or, more boldly, under the gas lamp on the corner below his window. One night, a man in a dark overcoat stood on the edge of its circle of illumination, his head wreathed in cigarsmoke; but Bolton couldn't make out his features under the broad brim of his nondescript black hat. Wells, Fargo never forgets.

*　　*　　*

Less than a month after Bolton's impromptu press conference on the prison wharf, Company detectives assigned to his surveillance reported that he'd vanished from the Nevada House. He was said to have been seen in Modesto, California, buying a train ticket to Madera, with a stopover in Merced. The reports could not be confirmed, and nothing else was heard after the train left Madera for Fresno.

Nine months later, on November 20, 1888, a man wearing a flour-sack hood and carrying a shotgun relieved the Eureka–Ukiah stage—several times an old victim of Black Bart's—of seven hundred dollars in gold coin and eleven sacks of mail. The bandit left behind only bootprints—no evidence of horse's hooves—and a scrap of foolscap written on in coarse pencil:

*So here I've stood while wind and rain*
*have set the trees a-sobbin';*
*and risked my life for that damn stage*
*that wasn't worth the robbin'.*

# AFTERWORD

*My tale it is finished, and my race it is run;*
*but there's one more confession I owe everyone.*
*I speak not of inventions, though admit to this crime;*
*I own to the evils I've committed in rhyme.*

Well, I never claimed to be a poet; or even a "Po8" on the
scale of Bart. But the seductive alliteration of the book's title
called for some verses to justify the presence of the word
"ballad."

In the interest of reducing confusion, I've taken some
small liberties with fact as it applies to Charles E. Bolton,
né Boles, and known more infamously as Black Bart; but
the most implausible portions of the narrative are a matter
of historical record.

I am hardly unique in playing fast and loose with some
of the lesser details. Sources professing to be authentic con-
tradict one another over such things as the names of Boles's
wife and daughters, and where he was born. One in particular provides two different addresses for both the Webb
House and Thomas Ware's tobacco shop, without claiming
to be in confusion on the matter; they change without

explanation. This is sloppy research, and I cherry-picked my way through it hunting down bits I could swallow, backing up what I could from other sources. The historical novelist has the privilege of improvisation and invention; the historian does not.

I have applied creative license mostly to the investigating part of the narrative. Criminal forensics (and Bart's is at least half a detective story) is a tedious business outside the world of entertainment, characterized by routine and repetition and complicated by false leads, bad tips, and unreliable eyewitnesses; it benefits from some telescoping in the retelling. Aside from such embellishments as appeal to the dramatic, the efforts of James B. Hume, Harry Morse, Benjamin Thorn, and others to identify and apprehend Black Bart are as reported. Sherlock Holmes brought nothing to the science of criminology that wasn't already there.

Where Charles E. Bolton is concerned (with the single exception of a *Pilgrim's Progress*–like journey to the site of his domestic past—there's no evidence it took place, but the melodramatist in me couldn't resist), I've clung as scrupulously as possible to historical fact. (In the interest of balance, I sent James B. Hume off on a similar journey through the gold country, seeking to increase his knowledge of his adversary. Although there is nothing in the record to support this, it seems entirely within his method, and presents him with the prize of personally having retrieved the storied handkerchief; if I vouchsafed to allow Bolton the mercy of revisiting the haunt of his family desertion, I felt I should make a similar concession to his nemesis.)

Reality is by necessity hard to accept. As Mark Twain said, "Of course truth is stranger than fiction; fiction has to make sense." That a middle-aged man traveling almost entirely on foot should manage to rob a national banking concern twenty-eight times over the course of eight years—with an empty shotgun, no less—before tripping himself up on something as trivial as a misplaced handkerchief would never fly in the rigid world of pure fantasy. Yes, he was as elaborately polite in the commission of his felonies as represented; yes, he acted without accomplices. And yes, he left some cheeky lines of doggerel at the scenes of robberies. This, even more than his astonishing record of success, guaranteed him a unique place in legend.

He was no Robin Hood, mind; he robbed from the rich and gave to himself. Worse, he abandoned his wife and family, and for this indecency we must withhold pardon; but Paul Gauguin did the same in order to pursue his art, and history has forgiven him for the sake of his genius. Some daubs on canvas may outlast one's sins; but so too many a romantic legend. If we are to commute a painter's sentence because of his skill and talent, we should review a nonviolent highwayman's record in view of his own unique gifts.

Of Bolton's life after he vanished from the Nevada House following his incarceration, we know next to nothing, theories notwithstanding. (He was reported to have exported his larcenous talents to such exotic places as Japan, China, and Australia.) He may have been responsible for a number of later stagecoach robberies that matched his *modus operandi*; James B. Hume seemed convinced that he was, although he later recanted, possibly for the simple reason that a thief-catcher is loath to admit that his thief is again at large and back to his old ways despite his drubbing. Wells, Fargo's able chief of detectives remained in his position long after he'd achieved his greatest public triumph: he oversaw the recruitment of Wyatt Earp, just the kind of shoot-first-and-ask-questions-later lawman he distrusted, as an undercover operative for the Company throughout Earp's turbulent time in Tombstone, Arizona—and with the decline of valuable stagecoach shipments in a settling West shifted his attention to train robberies. He continued in his position for many years until failing health forced him to retire.

Rumors surfaced that a shotgun-wielding masked bandit gunned down by a shotgun messenger during an attempted robbery on the run between Virginia City and Reno, Nevada, in the summer of 1888 was Bolton. The man was buried mere yards from the spot where he expired, in a grave soon obliterated by wind, rain, and dust, and now impossible to locate. If this was indeed the finish of Black Bart, it would eliminate him as a suspect in the "wasn't worth the robbin'" raid the following November. In any case, no record of Bolton's existence extends beyond that year.

To my knowledge (and with apologies to those who may have made the effort, which I failed to notice), this singular chapter of frontier history has never before been recounted in dramatic terms. In 1948, Dan Duryea—a talented and overlooked actor in westerns and films noir—starred in a programmer entitled *Black Bart,* but the storyline bore no resemblance to the more fascinating reality. In those days, with a few notable exceptions, frontier fiction on-screen and in print favored spirited gunplay, midnight rides, and fleeting romance over authenticity, superior though it was to the fevered imaginings of screenwriters on contract. In any event I thought it high time the man had his day.

"Black Bart" acted partly from revenge, partly from a

yearning for the finer trappings of wealth. He paid his debt to society—when it came due—and walked away from prison essentially unchanged by his four years and two months in incarceration. This was no small feat in those pre-rehabilitory days of inhuman punishment, barely sufficient meals, and sundry other atrocities unspeakable even today, which shattered the will of many a more obstreperous inmate. And he never took a cent from an individual, preying instead upon a commercial enterprise as large as some countries of the world. In view of recent discoveries regarding the practices of Wells, Fargo & Co. in our own day, one might ask, along with Bart: "After all, why *not* rob a bank?"